"I need to know...

"Did my *eldre* force you to agree to work with me?"

He looked so concerned, so she smiled softly. "David, they didn't force me to accept. I am pleased to cater your family reunion. *Oll recht?* Don't worry about it. I know this can't be easy for you."

He nodded. "The thought of spending time with all those people I don't know who are related to me... Frankly, it scares me."

Fannie reached out to place her hand over his. "I'll be there, and you know me. You'll get the chance to know me better when we plan this." She saw his surprise and felt his shock as he stared at her hand on top of his. Embarrassed, she quickly withdrew it. "Sorry."

David looked up and their gazes connected. "Why?"

She felt her face heat. "I overstepped."

He grinned. "*Nay*. You made me feel better."

Still, she didn't want to think about the way she'd automatically reached for his hand. As she had done before...when they were courting.

Rebecca Kertz was first introduced to the Amish when her husband took a job with an Amish construction crew. She enjoyed watching the Amish foreman's children at play and swapping recipes with his wife. Rebecca resides in Delaware with her husband and dog. She has a strong faith in God and feels blessed to have family nearby. Besides writing, she enjoys reading, doing crafts and visiting Lancaster County.

Books by Rebecca Kertz

Love Inspired

Loving Her Amish Neighbor
In Love with the Amish Nanny
The Widow's Hidden Past
His Forgotten Amish Love

Women of Lancaster County

A Secret Amish Love
Her Amish Christmas Sweetheart
Her Forgiving Amish Heart
Her Amish Christmas Gift
His Suitable Amish Wife
Finding Her Amish Love

Lancaster County Weddings

Noah's Sweetheart
Jedidiah's Bride
A Wife for Jacob
Elijah and the Widow
Loving Isaac

Visit the Author Profile page
at LoveInspired.com for more titles.

His Forgotten
Amish Love

Rebecca Kertz

LOVE INSPIRED
INSPIRATIONAL ROMANCE

ISBN-13: 978-1-335-58706-0

His Forgotten Amish Love

Copyright © 2022 by Rebecca Kertz

For questions and comments about the quality of this book, please contact us at CustomerService@Harlequin.com.

Love Inspired
22 Adelaide St. West, 40th Floor
Toronto, Ontario M5H 4E3, Canada
www.LoveInspired.com

Printed in U.S.A.

LOVE INSPIRED
INSPIRATIONAL ROMANCE

LOVE INSPIRED®

INSPIRATIONAL ROMANCE

Recycling programs
for this product may
not exist in your area.

ISBN-13: 978-1-335-58706-0

His Forgotten Amish Love

Love Inspired
22 Adelaide St. West, 41st Floor
Toronto, Ontario M5H 4E3, Canada
www.LoveInspired.com

Printed in U.S.A.

Chapter One

❧

*Summer, Lancaster County,
Pennsylvania*

"**I** wiped off the tables and put the dishes in the dishwasher."

Fannie Miller smiled at her employee, Linda King, as the young woman entered the kitchen from the front dining room of Fannie's Luncheonette. "*Danki*, Linda. *Wunderbor* job today."

Linda smiled. "We were slammed, weren't we?"

"*Ja*, but we did *oll recht*," Fannie said, and Linda nodded. "Why don't you head home?"

Frowning, Linda approached where Fannie stood at the kitchen work counter. "Aren't you leaving, too?"

"*Nay*, not yet. I have some baking to do for tomorrow." Fannie dumped flour into a bowl and then added a cup of sugar. "I won't be long, though, then I'll leave." She smiled. "Here—take this dessert home to your family."

"Fannie…"

"Please, it's fine. I appreciate everything you do for me. Enjoy it. It's a *snitz* pie." It was one of Fannie's favorite pies to make. The treat called for dried apples that were soaked in water and then put through a colander until they reached a soft texture like applesauce. The mixture was then combined with sugar and seasonings, placed between two piecrusts and baked.

She loved cooking and was determined to grow her business. She cracked an egg into the bowl and then added two more.

"Linda, I'd like the luncheonette to offer catering services."

Linda appeared thoughtful. "We'll need help if you do."

"*Ja*, I'll have to hire at least two extra full-time employees." Catering would be the perfect way to mingle with the community while providing a service. Hiring one or two new employees would be well worth it in the end. Fannie beat the eggs with a fork. "So, what do you think? It might be difficult for a while until we get used to the work."

"Sounds like a fine idea to me. I love a challenge." Linda grinned and then lifted the pie. "*Danki* for this, Fannie."

"You're more than *willkomm*. Have a *gut nacht*. Tell your *mam hallo* from me."

"Will do. The same to you." With dessert in hand, the young woman left through the back entrance of the restaurant.

Fannie mixed several more ingredients for lemon cake and then poured the batter into two cake pans before she placed them in the preheated oven. She set the timer for thirty-five minutes. Enjoying a cup of tea while she waited, she found her thoughts wandering to the space on the second floor of her building. If she converted the upstairs into an apartment, she could move out of her father's house, giving him the privacy he deserved with his new wife. And living on-site at Fannie's would afford her the convenience of simply heading downstairs to get an early start on food preparation each day.

The timer rang, signaling the cakes were done. Fannie took them out to cool. *I'll add frosting early tomorrow morning.* She'd already made two pies—apple crumb and shoofly—and a pan of chocolate-chip brownies with fudge frosting. This morning, she'd plated the cake, brownies and slices of each pie. While her lemon cakes baked, Fannie had cleaned up her mess and then turned on the automatic dishwasher. The appliance had come with the building she'd rented a year and a half ago before she bought it earlier this year. The owner wanted to sell, and business had been good enough to give her the capital needed.

Reaching for the "specials" menu for the next day, Fannie glanced over her list and decided she'd have enough time to get the food ready tomorrow morning with Linda. Having her as an employee was a blessing. The young woman was her stepmother's niece, and she would always be grateful that Alta had suggested Linda as a possible hire after Fannie had confessed that she needed help. Linda's sister, Esther, also assisted part-time, whenever she wasn't busy with her housecleaning business. Fannie was pleased with the sisters' work and her growing customer base.

As she cleaned the kitchen, Fannie heard the bells on the entrance door jingle as someone entered the building. With a frown, she realized that she'd forgotten to lock the front door. Leery, hoping that it wasn't someone who had come for nefarious reasons, Fannie grabbed her order pad while praying that it was only a late customer. She couldn't turn away a customer who wanted food.

She entered the dining room and saw a man seated at a table with his back to the front window. As if sensing her presence, he looked up from one of the menus she kept in a rack on every table. His eyes studied her with interest, and he flashed her a smile.

Fannie froze. She stared at him with her heart beating wildly.

David.

She knew his face and smile, and once she'd loved everything about them, about him. Those attractive features belonged to David Troyer, the man she'd loved. The man who had disappeared two years ago, the day after he'd told her he loved her and wanted to court her. That day had been a joyous occasion that turned bad the next afternoon when she learned that he'd left town with his family without a

word. The Troyers had never returned...
until now. Fannie had given up all hope of
seeing him again, but here he was—and
now what she needed was an explanation.

"Hallo," he said. "Is it too late to get a
sandwich?"

As she approached him, she saw no recognition in his expression. Fannie frowned.
"We were getting ready to close, but *ja*, of
course, you can get a sandwich or anything
else you'd like. What kind?"

"Roast beef—"

"On rye with mayo." She automatically finished for him, and he appeared
stunned that she'd guessed correctly. Only
she hadn't guessed. She *knew* because of
all those times they'd spent together in
secret, a young couple falling in love.
A time during which he'd bought sandwiches for them—roast beef on rye with
mayonnaise—before she'd meet him on
the street along the back edge of her father's property. Then he'd drive her in his
buggy to their favorite spot, park out of

sight, and they'd enjoy a leisurely picnic together.

"How did you know what I wanted?" He was grinning, and the way his blue eyes lit up tugged at her heartstrings.

She arched her eyebrows. "Experience," she said. "David, when did you get back into town?" Fannie fought to appear as if his presence didn't upset her.

He looked shocked. "You know me?"

Fannie frowned. "You don't remember me?"

"I'm sorry. I don't." He studied her as if her face would provide the answers to their questions.

Was he telling the truth? How could he forget after all they'd meant to each other? "You used to live in town. We met when your family moved into our church district." She held up her pad, shaken by the fact that he had forgotten her. "What would you like to drink? Iced tea? Soda? Coffee or tea?"

"Iced tea, please." David didn't take

his eyes off her, a fact that made her extremely uncomfortable.

Fannie jotted down what he wanted, then she turned to leave. She wanted to ask him what happened since he left, but something held her back. It was as if she recognized something broken in him.

"What's your name?" he asked, causing her to stiffen then halt.

She met his gaze and felt a flutter in her stomach. "Fannie."

"*Ach!* Fannie's Luncheonette. This place is yours." He eyed her intently but appeared pleased by her answer.

Despite the pain she'd endured since his disappearance, Fannie couldn't help a small smile. Before he'd left New Berne, there had always been something about him that had lifted her spirits.

What happened to you? Why don't you know me?

"I'll be out shortly with your order," she said, spinning away to hide the sudden tears that sprung to her eyes as she realized that this man—her former beloved—was not the same man he was before he'd left.

David watched Fannie head toward the back of the restaurant to get his order. She was beautiful with golden blond hair and sky blue eyes. A patchwork apron covered her light-blue tab dress, and he realized why. She'd been cooking—*nay*, baking, for he could smell the mouthwatering scent of lemon cake emanating from the back.

She remembered him. He couldn't recall whether he knew her or not.

Closing his eyes briefly, he struggled for a glimpse into his past. The doctor in the hospital had explained that he suffered from amnesia after a violent attack, but he had no recollection of it. According to his parents, his family had left New Berne two years ago and gone to New Wilmington after David's grandfather had hurt himself and become deathly ill.

During his grandfather's recovery, David had also ended up in critical care. Yet his mind remained blank. The only thing he could recall was when he'd first woken up in the hospital to people he didn't recognize. David eventually had become familiar with his family's faces, but there were still things about them he didn't remember...like his childhood.

After he and his grandfather had healed physically, his parents decided to return to the house where David had grown up, and they'd brought his grandparents with them. Living here again might trigger a spark in his brain that could bring back his past. At least that was what his *dat* believed. David hoped so. It was what he lived for now. Getting his memory back after all this time was his biggest focus. His neurologist told him not to force it, which frustrated him to no end. He felt like a stranger in his parents' home.

He'd felt cooped up since their arrival in town, which was why he'd decided to get out of the house and walk to Fannie's Luncheonette just up the road.

Fannie came out from the back, drawing his attention. She carried a glass of iced tea and a plate of food. He smiled at her as she placed it carefully in front of him. "I added some potato chips," she said. "I hope that's *oll recht*. I should have asked if you'd rather have potato or macaroni salad."

He glanced down at his sandwich and chips. His mother always kept a bag of potato chips on hand for him. He had no idea if he'd liked potato chips before the attack, but he certainly enjoyed them now. "This is perfect. I love potato chips. *Danki*."

"You're welcome," she said. Fannie left his table to flip the sign on the entrance door from Open to Closed. She started toward the back. "Please take your time. I have a few things to do in the kitchen."

"You were closed. I'm sorry. I shouldn't have come in." David felt bad for stopping by—and for not remembering her.

Fannie shook her head. "Please don't be. I've been baking, and I never mind providing food for a customer."

David smiled. *"Danki."* He picked up one half of his sandwich and took a bite. "This is delicious," he told her. "You cook the roast beef yourself? It doesn't taste as if it was purchased from a deli."

"Ja, I cooked it," Fannie said.

"I'll have to come back to try one of your specials." David gestured toward the simple sheet of paper tucked inside the rack of menus.

"We have different ones each day." She grinned. "Today's special was Amish chicken potpie. I would have offered you some, but we sold out by two."

"What's on tomorrow's list?" he asked, curious. He saw her glance briefly toward the back.

"Fresh baked macaroni and cheese as well as meat loaf stuffed with cheese." Fannie nodded. "I better get to work." She turned to leave him.

For some reason, he wanted her to keep him company while he ate, but he couldn't ask since she had things to do. "Fannie?"

She opened the door to the back. *"Ja?"*

"What's your last name?" he asked softly. "Mine is Troyer."

"I know." Some emotion that he didn't recognize flickered in her blue eyes. "Miller."

"Danki again, Fannie Miller, for feeding me this wonderful sandwich with chips that I love."

A smile teased at her lips, and she shook her head as if perplexed. "You're *willkomm*, David Troyer." Then she left for the kitchen.

As he ate his food, David studied his surroundings. There were tables in different positions around the room, some facing the rear of the store, while others had been placed alongside the windows so that diners could look outside while they ate. The tables and chairs were made of oak, probably handmade by an Amish cabinetmaker. There wasn't anything on the walls, but they had been painted a soft blue, much like Fannie's dress and eyes.

David picked up his iced tea glass and took a sip. The brew was tasty with the right amount of sugar and lemon. By the time he had finished his sandwich and drink, Fannie still hadn't come back to check on him. On a whim, he grabbed his empty plate and glass and then headed toward the door where he knocked, hoping that she'd answer.

Fannie opened the door and seemed stunned to see him with dishes in hand. "I'm sorry. I got caught up cleaning up my mess."

"You were busy and I intruded on your work." He gazed at her with warmth.

She bit her lip as she blushed. "You want dessert?"

"*Ja*, anything will be fine. And if you don't mind packing it up to go, I'll pay my bill and then leave you in peace."

She waved him to follow her after she'd

accepted the plate and cup from him. Curious, he trailed after her, wondering what he was doing in this restaurant with its pretty owner. She led him into the kitchen, which looked fresh and clean. He saw two cake layers cooling in their pans on wire racks. Fannie gestured toward a glass dessert case, where numerous treats tempted one to taste.

"I have chocolate cake," she said, pointing to small plates that held pieces of the dessert. "And brownies, shoofly pie and apple pie with crumb topping."

Everything looked wonderful. "May I have a piece of the apple pie?"

With a nod, Fannie met his gaze briefly then reached inside the case for a large piece of apple pie. David watched her lift the slice from the plate with a spatula and set it in a to-go box.

"Here you go," she said as she handed it to him.

"How much do I owe you?" he asked,

reaching toward his shoe where he'd put money earlier.

"Nothing," she said.

After straightening, David frowned as he shook his head. *"Nay,* I ate your food and now it's time to pay." He reached into his shoe and pulled out a paper bill.

She shook her head. "Please take the pie and enjoy the free meal."

"That doesn't seem right. I have the money to pay."

"I'm not taking it." She untied her apron and pulled it off. "I'll let you get it next time."

"Ach, I'll be back, no doubt about it." As he tucked his money away under his left suspender near his pants, David glimpsed her beautiful face, noticing her long dark eyelashes, unique in someone with blond hair. Her nose was perfect for her face, and her pink lips formed a lovely cupid's bow.

"Where are you parked?" she asked, averting her eyes from his study of her.

"I walked."

She appeared surprised. "I—ah—do you need a ride home?"

David grinned while he shook his head. "*Nay*, I enjoy walking and it's not far."

"You can exit through the back. Follow me." Fannie left the kitchen for a long corridor that ran from the dining room to the back entrance. Besides the kitchen door, David saw three other doors off the hallway as he kept up with her brisk pace to the rear of the building. She turned the knob and pulled the door open for him. She seemed to hesitate. "David, did something happen to you?"

He felt a jolt. "I...*ja*." But he couldn't talk about it right now. David wanted to enjoy one day without his amnesia getting the better of him. Why couldn't he recall Fannie, who recognized him as a church member?

"Do you want to talk about it?"

"There's nothing to share," he said, his mouth tightening.

A flicker of hurt passed over Fannie's features but then was gone so fast, he thought he'd imagined it. "Have a *gut nacht*, David," she whispered.

"*Gut nacht*, Fannie." He started through the door and then halted as a wave of familiarity about her washed over him. He had the sudden urge to get to know her. "Fannie, would you like to have a meal with me sometime?" he asked impulsively.

Her blue eyes filled with sadness as Fannie gazed at him for a long time. "*Danki*, David, but I can't." He saw her swallow hard. "This place keeps me busy."

David nodded, accepting the rejection because he shouldn't have asked her, not with his past a blank slate that needed to be filled. As he left, he wondered what— or who—had put that look of sorrow in her pretty eyes. Maybe he'd ask her one day after his memory returned. *If it ever returns.*

Fannie Miller was a beautiful woman with a kind soul. She refused to allow him to pay for his meal. He'd have to think of a way to make it up to her. He had no idea how. She didn't need a man who had a piece of him missing.

As he walked toward his family home, David took in his surroundings. God had given him many blessings. He was alive after being near death, and he had his parents, siblings and grandparents who gave him support and assurance during those times when he became frustrated with his situation.

He paused in his tracks and closed his eyes. *Someday.* Someday he prayed that he'd be mentally strong enough to have a relationship.

As he walked up the lane to his parents' house, David wondered why such fanciful thoughts of a woman he'd just met affected him so strongly. He shook his head and forced the images of Fannie Miller from his mind.

Chapter Two

"**D**avid, where have you been?" his mother asked as he entered the house.

"I took a walk," he said. "I told Mary I was going."

"Where?" His *mam*'s expression held concern.

Would his parents ever stop worrying about him? He was healthy and had only gone down the road. True, it was some distance from here to the restaurant but it was a straight shot, and he couldn't get lost. He understood his parents' concern for him. It wasn't every day that a man was beaten to within an inch of his life.

David had spent a full week in the hospital and then months seeing his doctors, including a neurologist, since he'd woken up without his memory.

"I went to Fannie's Luncheonette down the road." He regarded his parent with love. "It isn't far. You remember seeing it, *ja*?"

"*Ja*. I remember." His *mam*'s expression softened. "Did you eat there?"

"I did. Had a roast beef sandwich with potato chips. So *gut*, Mam. You and Dat should try the food there." He smiled at her. "And I brought home some apple pie with crumb topping if you'd like to share it with me. It looks delicious!" He opened the take-out box to show her the huge slice that Fannie had given him.

"That pie does look *wunderbor*," she agreed. "I'd like to have a taste of it."

David grinned and went to a kitchen drawer to take out two forks and a knife, then he reached into a top cabinet for two small plates. He cut the pie into two equal pieces then he gave one to his mother and took the other slice for himself.

They sat across from each other at the kitchen table, enjoying their treat in silence for a time.

"Where is everyone?" David asked finally.

"Dat is at Kings General Store asking about hiring someone to do renovations for us. Grossmudder and Grossvadder have trouble with stairs so it's best to add another bedroom on the ground floor for them."

David frowned. "Why not simply build them a *dawdi haus*? We have the yard space."

"Maybe Jed King will suggest it," Mam said before she ate another forkful of pie.

He decided to bring up a sensitive subject. "Mam, I know you and Dat worry about me. It must have been hard to see me banged up and my not recognizing you and Dat or my siblings when I woke up in the hospital. But, Mam? I'm doing better now. I remember all of you and now parts of this town. Going to the restaurant might seem like a risk to you but not to me. It was a bit of a stroll, but it's on the same road as our *haus*."

Mam studied him with tears in her eyes. "It was terrible, David. I never want to see you hurt again. I—we were afraid we'd lost you…"

He reached across the table to settle his hand over hers. "But you didn't, so *Gott* must have a different plan for me, *ja*?" David lightly squeezed her fingers. "And we still have Grossdaddi and Grossmudder although we all thought Grossdaddi was on his deathbed. We have been truly blessed." He withdrew his touch and smiled. "Life is *gut*. Let's trust in the Lord that everything will be fine." Putting his faith in God was what he needed to do. His goal was to get back his memory and then live a normal life with a wife and children.

"Okey." His mother nodded. "This is delicious. Tell me about this eatery."

"Fannie's Luncheonette," he said. "It's run by Amish."

"Fannie..." Mam looked thoughtful. "Fannie Miller?"

"Ja, do you know her?" David was surprised that she knew the owner's name, but then he guessed she knew most of the people in New Berne after having lived here for many years before their time in New Wilmington.

Mam smiled. "From what I recall, Fannie is one of Jonas Miller's *dechter.* Jonas runs a dairy farm."

"Did I know her?" David asked, curious. "Do you know what she looked like?"

"You most likely met her from church, if it's the same young woman. Jonas has five children. I know that his wife passed on five or six years ago." She looked thoughtful. "Fannie could be the girl who looks like her *mudder.* Blond hair. Sweet girl." His mother rose to put on the teakettle before she returned to her seat. She ate another bite of the dessert. "The pie is *wunderbor*. I think I'll suggest to your *dat* that we stop at Fannie's for lunch sometime."

David planned to eat there again, not only because of the food he'd enjoyed. He also wanted another chance to see Fannie.

Fannie exited the kitchen after she'd put away the lemon cake she'd made. She entered the dining area to wipe off the table where David had eaten. Seeing him again had caught her off guard. Pausing, she briefly closed her eyes. *David Troyer.* The man she'd loved and lost. He was back in New Berne and didn't recognize her. Or was he pretending he didn't know her because he no longer cared? She blinked back tears. What should she do now? Forget what they'd once meant to each other?

Fannie should have pushed for an answer as to why he'd confessed his love for her before he suddenly disappeared for two years without a letter or phone call. Two years of not knowing where he was and still she hadn't forgotten him…and all the outings they'd gone on secretly until finally he'd requested to officially court her out in the open. She'd been happy. Fannie had gone to bed that night with her spirits high and her heart full.

And then everything had changed the next day when she and David were supposed to meet and he didn't show. Upset, she'd gone to his house and found it empty. The whole family was gone. Fannie had waited for days, going back to check if David had come home, but he never had. Finally, after weeks of hoping, Fannie realized that the family must have moved. The Samuel Troyer family was gone, and no one knew where they went or why. The Troyers' first missed Sunday church service had prompted Fannie to ask the Troyers' closest neighbor, Evan Bontrager, about the family's whereabouts. Evan hadn't known why they'd left, but he suspected that there must have been a family emergency for them to leave so quickly and without a word. He'd been as perplexed as she that they hadn't returned.

Not long afterward, a new family to the area, the Paul Stoltzfuses, had come to church and were introduced to the community. The family had moved into the Troyers' residence, where they'd lived for nearly a year. It was only after the Stoltzfus family had moved out of the house a few weeks ago that Fannie realized they must have rented the place from Samuel Troyer.

Trying unsuccessfully to force thoughts of David away, Fannie briskly sanitized the table. As she wet-wiped the chair where David had been sitting, she saw something lying on the floor beneath the table close to his chair. She bent to pick it up and saw that it was a crumpled ten-dollar bill. *He must have dropped it.* She tucked it beneath the edge of her apron. What should she do with it?

Return it to David. She knew where he lived. The house was a mile or two down the same road as her restaurant. Fannie did one final check around the dining room to see that everything was clean and ready for the next day.

She went back to the kitchen and realized that the cake was cool. *I can put it in the dessert case and frost it first thing or I can ice it now and then put it in the dessert case finished and ready to serve.* Fannie pulled out the ten-dollar bill and placed it on the ledge above her worktable. *I'll return it after I finish the cake.* Fannie knew that working on the dessert now was her way of procrastinating because she didn't want to visit David's house to give him back his money.

I can't help it. I want to see him, but I'm afraid, too. I'm not ready yet.

Fannie whipped up a batch of homemade vanilla frosting and then spread it between the cake layers and over the top and sides. It didn't take as long as she thought it would. Or maybe it didn't feel that way because she dreaded seeing David again.

She enjoyed the extra time it took to wash the frosting bowl and the mixing utensils by hand. Another procrastination. Soon, Fannie couldn't avoid locking up and leaving.

Grabbing the money, she left the building and headed to her buggy. Her heart thundered in her chest as she climbed in, set the money on the floor on the passenger side of the vehicle and then drove out of the parking lot. A left turn got her headed in the right direction toward the Troyer house. Feeling emotional, Fannie swallowed against a lump in her throat as the residence came into view. She drove onto their dirt driveway and parked some distance from the house. Hesitating, afraid to knock on the door, she sat for a long moment in her vehicle, trying to garner the courage to get out.

Someone exited the barn and headed toward the house. Fannie recognized Samuel Troyer, David's father. He stopped as soon as he saw her buggy. She picked up the money and got out as he started in her direction.

"Samuel," she said. "I'm Fannie Miller. I own the restaurant down the road. David stopped in for something to eat, and when I was cleaning up afterward, I found this." She handed the ten-dollar bill to him. "Would you please give it to him?"

"Fannie." The man smiled, and David's resemblance to his father was evident in the curve of his lips and the warmth in his blue eyes. He wore a short-sleeved maroon shirt with black suspenders and navy tri-blend trousers with bulky black work boots. "You're Jonas's *dochter, ja*?"

"I am." She returned his smile. "You're back in New Berne... You've been gone a long time."

His expression sobering, Samuel inclined his head. "*Ja*, we didn't expect to be away from home this long."

"*Willkomm* back." Fannie glanced toward the house. "It's nice to have you in New Berne again." She was disappointed that he didn't offer the reason why they had stayed away, and it felt wrong for her to pry.

Samuel rolled back on his heels and then straightened. "*Danki.*" He held up the money. "And *danki* for returning this for David."

"I should go." Relieved that she wouldn't have to see David again so soon, she glanced toward her vehicle.

"Would you like to come inside and give the money to him yourself?" David's father asked.

"*Nay.* I appreciate the invitation, but it's been a long day, and I do need to get home." She looked toward the house and saw a curtain move in the upstairs window overlooking the driveway. Fannie caught a glimpse of a figure through the glass. *David.* Her heart thumped hard. She needed to leave. Now.

"Stop by again, Fannie." Samuel reached up to scratch a bare cheek above his gray beard.

Fannie gave him a small smile before she headed back to her buggy. Once she was on the road toward home, she breathed a sigh of relief.

Church Sunday came with sunshine and a light breeze. Fannie had dressed for service, and now she waited out in the barnyard. The last couple of days at work, she had been startled every time she heard the bells on the luncheonette door. Each time the jingle filtered into the kitchen area she felt an increase in her heart rate and a tightening in her stomach. Linda had been helping every day as usual. Fannie had asked her to take care of any new customers who entered. And she'd even taken a quick peek into the dining room to see if one of the diners was David. Thank the Lord that he'd never come back.

Her father exited the house and smiled

when he saw her. Preacher Jonas Miller was a good man, and she felt blessed to have him for her *dat*. Alta, his new bride, came out of the house then shut and locked the door. She was happy for them since they'd both lost their first spouses and were given a second chance at marital happiness.

Fannie had made potato salad and two apple pies for the shared midday meal after service. "Are you ready to go?"

Her *dat* nodded. "I've selected the reading and my sermon is prepared."

Alta smiled warmly at Fannie then looked with love at her husband. She carried a container of cupcakes, her favorite thing to make that everyone appreciated.

Fannie climbed into the back where she'd placed her food donations earlier and waited while her father and Alta got in the front seat of their family buggy.

"You look lovely," Alta said, turning around to meet Fannie's gaze.

Fannie grinned. "We're wearing the

same thing." Alta and she were both dressed in their Sunday best of royal blue dresses with a white cape and apron, two garments that appeared to be one full-length apron. They each wore a white head covering, and while Fannie usually wore a black *kapp* because she was unmarried, she'd chosen to wear a white one made of organza on a hot summer's day like today. Her Amish community was lenient in this regard, for which Fannie was thankful.

Service was being held at the Adam Kings, Alta's sister and brother-in-law's house. Fannie worried about the day—seeing David again, if he came, which she felt sure he would since the Troyers belonged to the same church district.

By the time they arrived, members of the congregation were already heading into service. Fannie didn't have a moment to prepare herself for seeing David, although she'd thought about nothing but him since his visit to her restaurant. After entering the barn, the space large enough to accommodate all members of their church, she followed Alta to the women's section. She and her stepmother sat directly behind Lovina, Alta's sister, as well as Lovina's daughters, Linda and Esther.

Fannie refused to look toward the men's section as the service started with a hymn. She'd been heartbroken when David left. Seeing him in her eatery the other day had jarred her.

The church elders left to meet in counsel for a few minutes, returning only after they had discussed whatever they needed to talk about. She saw them enter the barn and head to their seats. Watching her *dat*, she felt blessed to have a wonderful, caring father, who was always there and had an active role in her and her siblings' lives. As he stood near his seat close to the pulpit, Fannie caught sight of David. He was in the first row of men behind the elders, standing next to his father and his much younger brother, Simeon. David's eyes locked with hers and she looked away, her heart racing. Focusing her attention on the service to calm herself, she sang the selected hymns and listened to sermons. Once church was over, she quickly slipped out of the barn and hurried toward the house to help with the food.

Women were already in the kitchen. Fannie went to the refrigerator to take out her homemade potato salad, then she set it on the kitchen counter for a quick stir with a spoon.

"It was a nice service," a woman said as she entered the house. "I'm glad to be back with our church congregation."

With a glance in the newcomer's direction, Fannie recognized the familiar face. Alta, who accompanied the woman, waved Fannie over. "You must know Joanna Troyer? She and her family recently moved back to New Berne after being gone for a couple of years." She smiled as she gestured to Fannie. "Joanna, meet Fannie Miller, my *dochter*."

Fannie warmed to her stepmother who made sure she felt like an important member of the family.

Joanna studied her with kind eyes. "Fannie Miller—you own Fannie's Luncheonette?"

"*Ja.*" Fannie was surprised. "You've seen it?"

The woman nodded. "I have, but it was David who told me how *gut* it is."

"David?"

"My *soohn*. I believe he was your last customer on Thursday." Joanna smiled. "He had nothing but *wunderbor* things to say about your food. He shared your apple pie with me. I don't think I've ever had any that was so tasty."

Fannie grinned. "I'm glad you liked it. I brought two with me today."

"Fannie, would you help me take food outside?" Lovina asked as she entered the room and went straight to the refrigerator. "It's a lovely day, so the men are setting the tables up in the backyard."

"I'll be happy to." Fannie grabbed the two dishes that Lovina had pulled out of the refrigerator and placed on the counter. She carried them outside to the tables that had been set up for the food. After she put them on the closest one, she headed back toward the house. Suddenly, someone blocked her way. Fannie looked up. "David."

"Fannie," he said with a smile. "It's nice to see you again."

She shifted uncomfortably. "*Gut* to see you, too." David narrowed his gaze as if he didn't believe her. Fannie managed to smile convincingly to reassure him. Stunned by her mixed feelings for him, she bit her lip. "I saw your *mam* inside. She told me you shared the apple pie with her."

He nodded. "I did. It was delicious. I can't wait to go back to your luncheonette and try some of your specials and desserts."

"I brought potato salad and pies today,"

she said as she glanced behind him toward the house.

"I'm eager to try them." He readjusted his wide-brimmed black felt hat on his head. He looked good in his Sunday best—white shirt, black vest, black trousers and dress shoes.

"I should get back." Fannie managed another smile. "We still have a lot of dishes to bring out." When he nodded, she headed toward the house.

"Fannie!" he called.

She halted and glanced back at him. *"Ja?"*

He looked concerned. "We can be friends, can't we?"

Friends? She'd wanted so much more with him once, but losing him had changed all that. She refused to give her heart to anyone ever again. *"Ja,* we can be friends, David."

Then she turned and went into the house with emotions clogging her throat and hurting her heart.

Chapter Three

"Fannie!"

Fannie halted on her way to her family's buggy and spun to see who had called her name. She narrowed her eyes and recognized the young woman who approached. "Is that you, Mary Troyer?"

"Ja." David's younger sister grinned. "I wanted a chance to talk with you alone after service today, but there always seemed to be someone around."

Returning Mary's grin, Fannie met her halfway in the yard. "It was a really busy day," she said. "It's *wunderbor* to see you again. Two years is a long time. You've changed some. We both have."

"We both do look different." Mary glanced around as if checking her surroundings. It was afternoon and everyone was packing up their belongings to go home. The men had already cleaned up the tables and benches, and the women were still inside.

Fannie remembered being friendly with Mary, who was two years younger than her, at singings and church services such as today. Studying the young woman now, Fannie noticed the striking resemblance between Mary and David. While Mary's hair was blond and David's brown, brother and sister shared the same blue eyes, nose shape and smile. Mary was the feminine version of her masculine, attractive older brother.

"I heard you opened a luncheonette with the best food," Mary said.

Fannie arched her eyebrows. "Where did you hear that?"

"David."

"David," Fannie murmured and then

frowned. "Mary, is there something wrong with your *bruder*? He introduced himself the day he came into my restaurant as if we'd never met before."

"I'm sorry." Mary glanced back at the house before meeting Fannie's gaze. She lowered her voice as if she didn't want anyone to hear their conversation. "A lot happened since we were here last."

"Like what?" Fannie reached up to tuck a stray blond hair beneath her head covering.

"Right before we left," Mary said quietly, "we'd received word that my *grossdaddi* was seriously ill after a fall in New Wilmington. The doctors didn't think he'd live out the week."

Fannie offered a look of compassion. "Your *grossdaddi*...did he...?"

"*Nay*, miraculously, Grossdaddi is fine." Mary played with her *kapp* string. "He pulled through with the help of *Gott*. We're grateful to have him and Grossmudder still with us. Before we came back to New Berne last week, my *mud-der* convinced them to move closer to us. We put their home on the market a couple of months ago, and it finally sold."

"You must be relieved your *grosseldre* are in *gut* health." A light breeze began to blow and Fannie tilted her head up a moment, enjoying the feel of it on her face.

"*Ja*, we are. But there was more to worry us while we were away. The day after we arrived in New Wilmington, Mam asked me to pick up a few groceries. David offered to drive me to the store. While I went inside, David waited in the buggy. It didn't take me long to buy what we needed." Mary paused and became teary-eyed. "As I headed back with the groceries, I saw David lying on the ground near the buggy." Her face displayed the horror of that day. "Someone had beaten him and left him for dead. It was bad. He had multiple injuries, including cuts, broken bones and severe bruising." A tear escaped to trail down her cheek. "He was unconscious when I found him. He suffered a head injury, and there was blood… too much blood. I've never been so scared in my life."

Fannie fought tears of her own as she drew a shuddering breath. *Poor David.*

"An employee, who'd exited the store to put trash into a dumpster, saw me bending over David. I screamed for help and he hurried over. The man called for an ambulance and waited with me until it arrived."

Her heart bled for what he and his family had endured. "Mary…" she murmured with compassion. She pictured the man she'd loved bloody and unconscious… appearing dead. Horror rose in her throat.

"The reason we stayed in New Wilmington until recently was not only because of Grossdaddi but for my *bruder*, too. David had surgery to relieve pressure on his brain. He spent over a week in the hospital, Fannie, then he woke up with amnesia. At first, his neurologist believed David's memory loss was the direct result of his head trauma. He was under doctors' care for over a year. Although he's recovered physically, there is much he still can't remember. His medical team suspects his problem at this point is emotional. My *bruder* might be blocking out the memory of whatever prompted the attack."

"*Ach nay*, Mary. I'm so sorry." Fannie's heart ached. No wonder he didn't remember her! If only she'd known the reasons why he'd left…but then it wouldn't have made a difference. She hadn't heard from him in years. And now she'd moved on. She was devoted to her restaurant, which had helped her survive the heartbreak of losing David.

A teenage boy headed in their direction. Mary saw him and said, "My youngest *bruder*, Simeon."

"Mary, Dat said that he'll be ready to leave soon," Simeon said before glancing at Fannie with curiosity. She judged him to be sixteen years old or a little younger.

Fannie would have seen him in church two years ago but not at youth singings because he would have been too young to go.

Fannie recalled David talking about his younger brother back when the two of them had enjoyed time alone together.

Mary introduced her to Simeon. Fannie and Simeon exchanged quick hellos before the boy returned to the house.

"Now you know why David doesn't recognize anyone." Mary gazed at David who had left the house to retrieve something from the back porch before going back inside.

"Mary," Fannie said, "*danki* for sharing with me." She understood now why David had left and hadn't returned until recently.

"The sad thing is he didn't want to leave home," Mary continued. "David asked our *dat* if he could stay, but my *vadder* explained how ill our *grossdaddi* was, and it could be our last time to see him. We left town in such a hurry." The young woman shook her head, her lips quivering as if she was thinking about everything terrible that had happened. "David and Grossdaddi were in the same hospital, but David ended up staying longer. When my brother was released from hospital care, we still couldn't go home to New Berne until his doctors told us that David was well enough to travel.

"But we still couldn't leave New Wilmington. There was work to be done on my grandparents' *haus* so they could sell it. Once it sold and everyone was well enough for the journey, we were finally able to come home. It's hard to believe how much time has gone by. I couldn't wait to return. There are so many changes here. I noticed your luncheonette up the road from us first. There are other new businesses and houses, too."

"*Ja.* I opened my business about a year and a half ago." Fannie placed her hand on Mary's shoulder. "I'm glad you're back and your lives are improving." No wonder she'd thought the house had been empty—because it had been. And then one day six months later, she'd seen a strange family in the yard. Fannie had thought the Troyers had sold their house, and she'd been devastated by the knowledge that the family was never coming back.

"Dat hopes that now we're home, David will remember our life here. It might take a while, but we are praying it happens."

"I'll keep all of you in my prayers." Fannie fought the pinprick of fresh tears. She didn't want Mary to see how emotional she was feeling. Fortunately, Joanna Troyer called her daughter back to the house.

Mary met her gaze. "Do you have a cell phone?"

Fannie nodded. "I need one for my business."

"I have one in case of an emergency," the young woman said. "Can we exchange phone numbers?"

"*Ja*. What's yours?" she asked, and then

with shaking fingers, she entered the number David's sister gave her. Then Fannie gave hers to Mary.

"*Danki*, Fannie. I'll talk with you again soon." David's sister left Fannie alone to process everything she'd learned.

Would David ever remember what they once were to each other? She was more than a little shaken. *Ach, David.*

She went to the buggy and climbed into the back. Closing her eyes, she offered up a silent request to God that all would turn out well in the end.

David left the house and headed toward his family buggy. He halted abruptly when he saw his sister, Mary, talking with Fannie Miller. All day long as he interacted with members of the New Berne church congregation, he felt something hovering on the fringe of his memory. And then his headache started. It seemed that whenever he tried to force a memory, his head hurt and there wasn't anything he could do for the pain. His neurologist's advice before he'd left New Wilmington came back to him.

You can't force yourself to remember, David. The memories will come when they are ready and not before.

Breathing deeply, David tried to relax. Would he ever feel like himself again? Normal? He waited while Fannie and his sister went their separate ways before he stumbled toward an Adirondack chair in the yard and sat down. Bending forward, he dropped his head into his hands. With closed eyes, he begged the Lord for assistance. It had been a difficult road to recall his family—his mother, father, siblings and grandparents. Waking up in the hospital without knowing anyone or why he'd been injured had been terrifying.

He felt the excruciating pain at his temples and along the back of his head. David sat with his head bowed, trying to ease his thoughts and relinquish the pain. But the ache wouldn't go away. He drew in a shaky breath, then held it before he released it slowly.

"David?" a soft feminine voice said.

He lifted his gaze and saw Fannie. She wore a worried expression. "Are you feeling *oll recht*?" she asked.

"A headache," he admitted with a grimace. "It will go away eventually."

"Would you like me to get you ibuprofen or should I run inside to tell your family?" Her blue eyes were intent as she studied him.

"No need to bother them. They'll be out soon enough." David tried to smile but he knew it fell flat. "*Danki*, but ibuprofen doesn't help when I get like this." He felt her hand settle on his shoulder.

"I wish I could do something," she murmured as she briefly rubbed his shoulder before abruptly pulling away. "I have an idea. I'll be right back."

David didn't have the energy to stop her.

Fannie returned within a short time. "Stay still. I'm going to put warm compresses on your neck and forehead. I believe it will help."

David felt the wet warmth over his nape and then felt her hold one against his forehead. His head still hurt, but the compress felt soothing and wonderful against his skin. Unfortunately, the heat faded too quickly and his headache continued to throb.

Fannie removed the compresses and he heard the sound of water. "I'm reheating these in a bowl of hot water." Within seconds, she had both hot towels in place.

David sighed as the heat softened the tightness in his neck muscles. "That feels *gut.*"

"David?" His father appeared by his side. "Are you hurting, *soohn*?"

David was afraid to say anything because he didn't want the pain to get worse.

"He is, Samuel," Fannie said in a hushed voice as she carefully lifted the compresses from his skin.

"Come then, David." His *dat* helped him to his feet. "Let's get you home."

"Samuel?" his mother asked. "Is he *oll recht*?"

"He will be, Joanna." He leaned on his father for support.

"Joanna, I hope David feels better," he heard Fannie say. "I used these towels as hot compresses. I'm not sure if it helped."

"It did," he whispered as he looked up to meet her gaze. "*Danki*, Fannie. I'll have to use them at home."

"I never thought of using heat in that way. *Ja, danki*, Fannie," his *mam* said. "I'm grateful for your quick thinking."

"You might continue with heat when you get home," he heard her say.

"We will." He felt his mother's hand on his shoulder. "Samuel, I'll meet you at our buggy. I'll be right there." There was a pause as he and his father started toward their buggy. "I'll take *gut* care of him," his mother continued while he was still within earshot, and then Fannie's response, "I know."

His father helped him into the back of their family buggy.

"I'm *oll recht*, Dat." David leaned against the side and closed his eyes while his sister and younger brother got into the bench seat next to him. Would he ever get better? He tried to free his mind of any stressful thoughts as he attempted to rest.

Still, it was Fannie's voice that stayed in mind. The image of her face. Her golden blond hair and her concern. He felt a warmth invade his chest and a slight easing of his headache.

David realized that he'd fallen asleep when a short time later Mary woke him. "Bruder, we're home." Her voice was gentle as she roused him from his nap.

He blinked. "I'm sorry I dozed off."

Mary frowned. "Dat said you had one of those headaches."

David nodded. "*Ja*. I guess I was trying

to remember too hard." And it had been a long day.

"You need to let your memory return naturally," his younger brother, Simeon, said.

He agreed in theory, but it was difficult when his mind was like a chalk slate with the answers to his life erased until it was nothing but a blank black.

"Let's get you inside," his father said, opening the door. His *dat* reached in to help him.

"I feel like a baby who can't do anything," David murmured. He was frustrated and scared. He knew he shouldn't push, but he needed to remember. His life was currently on hold. He wouldn't have peace of mind until he got his memory back. And then he could begin to live again.

His *dat* stayed beside him and helped him enter the house. David was pressed to sit in a chair while his *mam* rummaged through a top kitchen cabinet. With an exclamation of relief, his mother turned with a prescription bottle in her hand.

"Your pain medication," she said.

David frowned. "I don't want any. They make me feel fuzzy. Besides, the pain is better, but I feel exhausted."

She unscrewed the cap. "*Soohn*, it's just to give you a little relief."

"*Nay*, please," David said, remaining adamant. "I've had enough of those to last me a lifetime." He saw his mother blink back tears. "Mam, I promise I'm fine." He managed a smile. "Fannie's hot towels helped me to get through it sooner than usual."

She put the cap back on the bottle and then put it away. "Why don't I fix a hot compress then?"

"*Nay*, I'm *okey* now. I'm just tired." He always felt as if he could take a long nap once his headache dissipated.

"Then you'll lie down for a while?" Mam gazed at him with concern.

"*Ja*, I'll go up now." He passed her as

he headed toward the stairs, and Mam touched his arm lightly. "I worry about you, *soohn*."

"I know you do," he said. "*Danki* for everything you do and have done for me." He managed a smile for her. "We need to have faith that my memory returns and things will get better."

David wanted to believe it. He couldn't continue to have blank spots in his mind and could only hope and pray that being here in New Berne would open the doors to his past.

Chapter Four

Wednesday morning Fannie was in her restaurant earlier than usual after having slept little the night before. She couldn't stop thinking about what had happened to David. After he'd left town, Fannie's Luncheonette had been her salvation when she'd been hurt and broken. During the process of establishing her clientele, she'd found she loved serving her food to others and getting the chance to get to know people within her community.

Cooking had always been a blessing to her. Her mother's skills in the kitchen had been passable, but they hadn't been as good as Fannie's. After her *mam* died, Fannie had taken over the kitchen to feed her family. After her siblings had praised her abilities, she'd decided to use her talent to earn a living. Before her mother's death, her sister, Sadie, had married and moved to New Gretna with her husband. Her eldest brother, Joshua, after falling in love at nineteen, had wed a woman who was two years older. He and his new wife, Anna, had moved to a small Amish community up north in Manheim Township before moving to Arthur, Illinois, where Anna had been raised. Which had left her *dat* and her twin brothers, Danny and DJ, for Fannie to feed. When the twins had rented a house together after starting their joint business a year later, only she and her father resided in the house her parents had purchased when they were newlyweds.

If things had been different, she and David might have been wed, perhaps with their first child already. But God had thought to keep them apart. She blinked back tears of regret. Nothing would ever be the same again.

Fannie truly felt bad for David, and she wished him well in his recovery. There would always be a part inside her that cared for him. But she had rebuilt a new life for herself and couldn't take the chance that her heart wouldn't be broken a second time. David Troyer didn't remember her, and even if he had, she could no longer find room for him in her future. Her restaurant took nearly every moment of her time now. Fannie's Luncheonette made her happy, and she wasn't willing to give that up. So, while her original plans had included David Troyer as her husband and the father of her children…things had changed.

Fannie heard a key in the back door lock and glanced at the clock to find it was six thirty, when Linda usually came into the luncheonette. She would have to consider employing someone else if Linda's sister,

Esther, couldn't work enough hours to help during the busiest times of the week.

"*Gut* morning, Fannie!" Linda donned the apron that had hung on a wall hook inside the workroom. "You're here early."

"*Gut mariga*, Linda. I've been here since four thirty." Fannie gave her a small smile. "It was a long night, so I figured I'd get a start on the baking."

Linda moved into work beside her. "Something happen that kept you up?"

"Just had a restless night." She pulled over a bag of flour and measured what she needed for a pound cake. She had already made several different desserts and two coffee cakes.

"Do you want to talk about it?" Linda brought over the sugar canister and placed it within Fannie's reach.

"*Nay*, nothing to talk about." Fannie continued to assemble the ingredients for the cake with Linda's help. "Do you know if Esther can work today?"

"I have no idea. If you'll let me use your

cell phone, I'll call and ask her." Linda smiled when Fannie handed her the phone. The young woman stepped away to make the call and returned after a few moments. "Esther has a cleaning job this morning, but it's a small one so she can be in for the lunch crowd."

"Gut." Fannie cracked eggs into the bowl then added melted butter from a pan. "I may need to hire another full-time worker soon. I appreciate whenever Esther can help, and that won't change, but word of mouth has certainly increased the business for breakfast and lunch." She stirred the batter by hand. "Do you know of anyone who would like a job?"

"I can't think of anyone offhand, but I'll look into it and let you know."

Fannie watched with pride as Linda prepared three loaf pans for the pound cake. "You're a fine assistant, Linda. Do you like working here?"

"I do." Linda slid the pans closer to Fannie, who stirred in the few last-minute ingredients before she dumped a third of the batter in each pan.

After sliding the loaves into the preheated oven, Fannie straightened them. "I'm glad you like it here. I don't know what I'd do without you."

Linda grinned. "You'll never have to find out."

An hour and fifteen minutes later, they had six breakfast casseroles during the last stages of baking, and the lunch special menu was planned for the day. The tables were set with place mats, and silverware rolled in paper napkins. Everything was ready for their first customers as Linda unlocked the door.

Their first one was a favorite. The older Englisher entered and sat down in his usual seat by the front window. Fannie had already added a mug to the table setting, expecting him.

"Good morning, Harry." Fannie approached with her pad. She liked to wait on the man herself.

"Mornin', Fannie." Harry studied the menu she'd left at the table. "What have you got for me today?"

"The special is a breakfast casserole," she said. "You have your choice of sausage or bacon." She was patient as he read the menu carefully. Usually, no matter the special of the day, Harry ordered two scrambled eggs, sausage links and rye toast. "The usual?"

The man set down the menu and glanced up at her with a smile. "I'd like the sausage breakfast casserole, please."

Fannie concealed her surprise. "Coming right up. You still want coffee?"

Harry nodded, and Linda approached with the carafe of decaf, which she poured into his cup, and a pitcher of cream, which the man liked in his brew. He ate at Fannie's Luncheonette at least twice a week, on Mondays and Wednesdays, and sometimes more. "Thank you, Linda."

"You're most welcome, Harry." Linda turned her attention to Fannie. "The usual?"

"He wants the sausage breakfast casserole this morning. Right, Harry?"

"Right," the man said.

Linda raised her eyebrows slightly before she headed back to the kitchen to get him a slice of the dish.

While Linda was gone, Fannie pulled a chair out across from Harry. "Would you like a piece of coffee cake to take home?" She smiled at him. "On the house."

The man took a sip of his coffee before answering. "I can't take that without paying."

"You can because it's a gift." Fannie stood as Linda entered the room with Harry's breakfast. She looked at Linda. "Don't let him leave after paying for breakfast. I have something I want to give him."

Harry's eyes glistened with tears. "You are a fine woman, Fannie Miller."

Fannie laughed. "I'm glad you think so."

The entrance door jingled as new customers entered. Fannie glanced over with a ready smile that she had to work hard to keep in place after four members of the Samuel Troyer family entered and sat down at a table in the middle of the room. Only Mary was missing, and the young woman was no doubt staying home with her grandparents.

"*Gut mariga*, Fannie," Joanna greeted.

"*Gut* morning to you, Joanna. Samuel. David. Simeon." Fannie tried not to look directly at David but found her gaze pulled in his direction anyway.

Joanna beamed at her. "We decided to eat breakfast here at David's recommendation."

Fannie met David's gaze. "I'm glad you enjoyed your sandwich the other day."

David grinned. The sight of his good humor reminded her of how he'd been when they were together two years previously.

Fannie felt her lips curve into a grin. "We have a case filled with desserts this morning."

"We may have to buy some and bring them home for after lunch," Samuel said.

Fannie nodded and stepped aside as

Linda approached their table. "Linda will take your order. *Danki* for coming in today." Then she headed back to the kitchen, her heart pounding with the knowledge that she was going to find it hard to keep David from working his way into her thoughts too often. Her business, she reminded herself, that's what was important.

She was in the kitchen with the lunch menu when Linda returned. "Harry's breakfast with his senior discount is three dollars," Fannie said.

Linda nodded. "You're a softy, Fannie Miller. Generous to a fault."

"I make more than enough money. I can afford to think of those less fortunate than me." Fannie felt blessed. She'd worked hard, and the success of her business was her reward. It felt wonderful to give back to the community. Besides, she enjoyed her customers, especially those like Harry, who clearly loved eating at her luncheonette. She wanted to do what she could to make people like him happy. After placing the treat into a cardboard take-out box, she headed toward the front room and saw Linda hand him his check.

The Troyers sat at their table with drinks that Linda must have been quick to provide. Fannie glanced toward the family before she turned her attention to Harry. The man was counting out three ones for his breakfast. "But what about the coffee?" he asked. "I don't see it here."

"That's included in your bill." Fannie approached with a smile and the box. "Here you go, Harry. Enjoy your day. Come back and see us again."

Harry stood, a frail slip of a man. "I will. Thank you, Fannie. It's been a pleasure as always."

Fannie opened the front door for him. "See you again soon." She shut the door after Harry left. "Your breakfast should be right out." Her gaze encountered David's. He studied her with a thoughtful look as she passed by. She joined Linda in the kitchen and picked up two plates while her employee carried the others.

"Here you go," Linda said as she set plates of sausage before David's parents.

Fannie placed bacon casseroles before David and Simeon. "Please let us know if you need anything else. Does everyone have enough coffee or tea?"

"We're fine," David said. "*Danki*, Fannie."

She smiled. "Enjoy." Then she left the dining room to prepare the lunch specials.

Linda entered the kitchen moments later. "Samuel Troyer asked if we could box up three servings of bacon casserole for them to take home."

"Let me know when they are done with breakfast." Fannie pulled out three take-out boxes and placed them on the ledge above the worktable. "I'll dish them up right before they leave so they'll still be warm when they get home. I imagine they're for Mary and her grandparents."

"And, Fannie? Joanna Troyer would like

a private word with you." Linda put emphasis on *private*.

"Please tell her to meet me near the restrooms. I'll wait for her there." Fannie wondered what David's mother could possibly want with her.

"Will do. I'll tell her to go now." Linda grabbed the coffeepot and grinned. "I'll top off their cups." She left the kitchen for the front dining room.

Fannie waited in the hallway near the women's restroom for David's mother. She didn't have long to wait.

Joanna Troyer smiled as she approached. "*Danki* for taking the time to talk with me."

"It's fine," Fannie assured her. "I have a few minutes before I need to finish preparing for the lunch crowd." She frowned. "Is something wrong?"

Joanna smiled. "*Nay*, not at all. I'd like to ask you something, and I didn't want anyone else to hear until I know if it's *oll recht*."

Fannie studied Joanna and saw a lovely woman with brown hair and blue eyes like her eldest son. She wore a light blue dress with white cape and apron. As per Amish custom, Joanna's hair was covered by a white organza prayer *kapp*. "How can I help you?"

"Samuel and I have discussed having a family reunion at our home. We enjoyed our breakfast at your restaurant. Everything was lovely. We were wondering— do you offer catering?"

Fannie was surprised and pleased. "I thought about adding the service but haven't catered any events yet."

"Your food is delicious. I know I'm asking a lot...but will you provide the food for our family reunion? I know you'll do a fine job. We'd love it if you would."

"I'd be happy to if you're sure you want me to." Fannie felt giddy. Handling the Troyer reunion could open up doors for the catering side of her business. Even if she would have to see David again.

"For sure and for certain," David's mother said. "We definitely want you."

Fannie smiled. "*Okey*. When will you hold the reunion?" She definitely needed to hire another employee or two.

"We were thinking of early August. This will allow time to send out invitations and get responses." Joanna was grinning from ear to ear. "Wait just a second." She moved toward the dining room and waved over her husband to join them. "I know Samuel will be pleased as well."

"Well? Did she agree?" Samuel said, walking over. He offered Fannie a smile.

"*Ja!*" In her excitement, Joanna placed a hand on her husband's arm. "I know the reunion will be a huge success."

"And she'll help plan it?" Samuel asked.

Fannie felt a jolt. "You want me to *plan* the reunion?"

"We'd like you to help David plan it," Joanna said. "I'll make a list of those we want to invite. If you'd help our *soohn* with the menu and the invitations, we'd appreciate it. We have a lot going on with my *eldre*. We thought about waiting until after they were settled in their new house before holding this but then decided to continue with it." Sadness reached the woman's blue eyes. "I pray that seeing family members and old friends will trigger David's memory. It's hard for us to see him suffer. I—*we*—" she looked up at her husband "—worry about him. So please agree, Fannie. It would mean so much to us…and hopefully to David if seeing his cousins and other family restores his past."

Fannie didn't know what to say, but she could feel this couple's pain. And since she desired to get into catering, she knew she would have to do this—to work with David Troyer. The man she used to love but who had left and then forgotten her, even if it wasn't his fault. It should make her feel better to learn about the reasons he'd been gone—and the reason he'd forgotten her—but it didn't. Because she'd been devastated when he'd disappeared. How could she ever forget how destroyed she'd felt after the one person she'd trusted and loved, the man who had asked to court her after confessing the seriousness of his intentions, had vanished without a word? She hadn't been able to confide in anyone after it had happened. No one had known of her relationship with David, and she'd been glad—and still was—that no one had a clue. It would hurt worse to be questioned by family and friends—and to be viewed with pity.

"Does David know about this?" Fannie asked.

"Not yet." Joanna exchanged glances with her husband before meeting Fannie's gaze. "We'll talk with him when we get home. I'll be in touch after we do."

"We should get back," Samuel said. "Before our sons wonder what we're doing back here."

As Samuel and Joanna went back to their table, Fannie returned to the kitchen.

Thoughts of David invaded her mind, and Fannie knew she needed to keep busy to banish them—hopefully. Cooking, a saving grace whenever she was upset, was the perfect outlet for forgetting who was seated in her dining room, eating her food.

Linda approached her. "The Troyers have finished their meal and are ready for their takeout."

With a nod, Fannie cut three generous slices of the bacon casserole and placed each one into a to-go box. "Here you go," she said as she handed them to Linda.

Her employee left with the boxes and returned with several breakfast orders. "It's getting busy out there," Linda said.

"*Gut.* Do you need a hand clearing the tables?"

"*Nay*, I'm fine. I'm sure it will be busier for lunch and by then Esther will be here."

Earlier, Fannie had decided to make a beef pie with potato crust for lunch. Breakfast hours were from seven thirty until eleven thirty and lunch ran late from noon until three thirty, so she had plenty of time to create this special. Her beef pie recipe called for thinly sliced roast beef, butter, a head of cabbage, beef broth, onion and seasoned mashed potatoes. And that was just for the filling. More mashed potatoes, eggs, flour, milk and water were the ingredients for the crust. It was one of her favorite dishes to make and eat. She had made it so many times she could do it quickly and efficiently. Fannie had two pies baking in the oven an hour later and went to work on the final special for the day, her twin brothers' favorite—crispy fried chicken.

Yet despite doing the one thing she loved, she couldn't stop thinking about David and everything he'd gone through since he'd left town—and her—two years ago. Fannie knew she had to get a handle on her emotions. David Troyer. The last man she needed to complicate her life.

David enjoyed his breakfast but left feeling let down. Linda was pleasant, getting them whatever they needed, including the meals to take home to his sister and grand-parents. It wasn't the service that bothered him. It was the fact that he hadn't got-ten to interact with Fannie as much as he would have liked. He'd liked having her wait on him the last time he'd eaten at her restaurant. She'd been cordial this morn-ing, but she was quick to leave after she'd delivered his casserole. Fannie had barely made eye contact with him, which upset him more than anything. And he didn't have a right to feel that way.

"You're quiet, David," his father said as they left the parking lot after a quick stop at Kings General Store. His parents had made him go inside as if they feared that what had happened to him in New Wilm-ington would occur again if he waited in their family buggy.

"Do you have another headache, *soohn*?" Mam turned in her seat to study him.

He managed a smile for her. "*Nay*. I'm fine. Not to worry."

"You were right about Fannie's food."

Simeon turned on the bench seat to look at him.

"It is *gut*." David was glad his family agreed with him. "I think Mary and our *grosseldre* will enjoy their breakfast."

Mam nodded. "*Ja*. Did you see the specials board? She's serving crispy fried chicken and beef pie with a potato crust. Sounds delicious!" She glanced at his *dat*. "I was half tempted to go back for a late lunch. I haven't eaten beef pie in ages."

"I'm sure there will be other wonderful dishes we can enjoy soon." Samuel gave her a warm smile. "You're a *wunderbor* cook yourself."

Mam chuckled. "*Ja*, but there is nothing like enjoying someone else's food."

David sat back and closed his eyes. He didn't have a headache, but he felt exhausted. It seemed as if he tired more easily since he'd been hurt two years ago. His father drove onto their driveway and parked close to the house. His parents climbed out of the vehicle first, then

Simeon got out and finally David. "Mam, Dat, do you mind if I lie down? Not long. I know I have chores to do."

"Of course, *soohn*," his *vadder* said. "Do you want one of us to wake you up later?"

"Please." David stopped to say *hallo* to his sister and grandparents and to hand them their to-go boxes. "Breakfast from Fannie's Luncheonette. I think you'll enjoy it."

"*Danki*, David," his grandfather said.

"*Soohn*, before you head upstairs," his mother said, "your *dat* and I would like to talk with you a minute."

"*Okey.*" He was confused. What was so important they couldn't wait until after his nap?

Samuel gestured for him to follow them outside. "Your *mudder* and I have decided to host a family reunion. We've asked Fannie to cater it for us."

David glanced his mother's way briefly. "Her food is *wunderbor*. I'm sure she'll do a *gut* job." The thought of being surrounded by a bunch of people made him uneasy, but if his parents wanted to do this, he would figure out a way to cope.

"There will be much to do to get ready," his *mam* said. "I'll be needing your help with the menu and the invitations. We'll get you a list. Your *dat* and I have things we have to do for your *grosseldre*."

Confused, David frowned. "You want me to handle this without help?"

"Nay," Samuel said. "We found someone to help you—and it's not your *schweschter* or *bruder*."

David looked at each of his parents. "Who then?"

His father hesitated. "Fannie."

He frowned again. "Fannie agreed to work with me?"

"She did." His mother smiled. "Once we make a list of everyone we'd like to invite, you can meet with her."

"I see." David barely managed a smile. "I'm heading up for a rest. We can talk about this later."

Once in his room, which he shared with

Simeon, David lay on his bed and stared at the ceiling. Despite the exhaustion he felt, he couldn't stop his mind from spinning. Fannie and he were going to plan their family reunion? He had to make sure that Fannie was willing to work with him, that she hadn't been coerced into the extra work.

Why were his *dat* and *mam* hosting a reunion?

And then it hit him. His parents hoped that someone at the event would trigger him to regain his memory.

Frustration with his amnesia made it difficult for him to think straight.

He tossed and turned, trying to banish images in his mind. Memory flashes of the doctor and nurses after waking in the hospital. The shock he'd felt when he didn't recognize the people who claimed to be his family.

David knew his immediate family now. He'd spent enough time with them for him to become familiar with each one of their faces. Yet, he still couldn't recall much of his childhood except what his sister, Mary, and his brother, Simeon, had told him.

David knew he had to rest; he wasn't getting enough during the night. His lack of sleep was adding to his confusion. At first, his doctor suggested medication to help him. But he didn't want to rely on a prescription to cure his insomnia.

There was something just out of reach that he should know. It frustrated him that he couldn't grasp it.

Every night, he closed his eyes briefly and prayed that God would help him. David wanted peace and to be settled. He needed to have the chance to live his life with memories of his past.

He yawned. He shut his eyelids and tried to bring lightness into his dark mind. He imagined a nicer place. It was daytime, and sunshine cast a golden glow over an open field of wildflowers. He could almost detect their scent. Focusing on the image, he took deep, calming breaths, trying to relax his body…his limbs. A butterfly landed gracefully on a white flower before fluttering to a blue one. A hummingbird landed on a bright red wildflower, pausing to drink from its nectar before flying away.

The scene he conjured in his mind eased his distress, and when something dark tried to intrude, David breathed deeply to keep himself in the beauty of nature. A noise downstairs threatened to rip him from the peace, and then his imagination pulled in a pretty young blonde woman with eyes of sky blue. *Fannie.* He saw her in the field watching the butterfly with a soft smile on her face. And he slept, finally finding the rest he desperately needed.

Chapter Five

It had been days since David had come in to eat with his family, but Fannie still had a clear mental picture of the way he'd looked at her after she gave him his breakfast. His gaze had been filled with curiosity. The fact that he didn't know her still hurt her in a way she hadn't expected.

It was Saturday morning, and she was cooking at home for tomorrow's Visiting Day. Gabriel and Lucy Fisher were to host.

Fannie mixed up a large bowl of macaroni salad to share at the midday meal. She had a cake baking in the oven, and the air was rich with the scent of chocolate. Earlier Dat had asked her to make whoopie pies, which she planned to do next.

The back door opened, and her father stepped into the kitchen from outside. He approached and smiled when he stood alongside her. "That salad looks *gut*," he said. He sniffed. "Chocolate cake?"

Fannie moved the macaroni salad aside. "*Ja*, but don't worry. I'll make you your whoopie pies next."

"I know I mentioned whoopie pies," Dat said, "but make whatever is easier. I know I'll get them eventually."

Fannie's stepmother entered from the other room. "What will you get? And when?" Her green eyes twinkled as she approached her husband.

"Whoopie pies." Dat put his arm around her. "I suggested she make them for dessert, but I don't want her to work too hard on her day off."

"Fannie?" Alta said. "Can I help in any

way? With the whoopie pies? Or I can bake some cupcakes. What do you think?"

"I love your cupcakes," Fannie heard her father say.

"Is it *oll recht* if I make cupcakes for us to bring?" She turned to Fannie. "You're always so generous to us. To me," Alta said softly.

Fannie looked at her stepmother with a smile. "It's easy to be generous to you, Alta. You make my *vadder* happy."

Her father beamed at her. "You're a *gut dochter*, Fannie." He kissed his wife's cheek. "Now that you are both busy in the kitchen, I'll get back to work. Nate has the day off. I have to set up the machines for milking." Then he left the house for the barn.

Half an hour later the cupcakes were in the oven, and Alta had put on a kettle for tea. A knock on the door drew Fannie's attention. She opened the door to see David Troyer on the doorstep. She felt a jolt in the center of her chest. The last person she'd expected to see was him.

He smiled at her. "*Hallo*, Fannie."

"Would you like to come in?" She stepped back to allow his entry.

"*Danki.*" David came into the kitchen, with its cluttered kitchen countertop and worktable displaying her mess from cooking. He glanced about the room. "It smells *gut* in here."

"I've been baking all morning." She wondered what he wanted. It seemed odd that he would stop by the house. How did he know where she lived? It certainly wasn't because he'd remembered.

He tilted his head and briefly closed his eyes. "Chocolate cake?" He met her gaze. "For Visiting Day?"

"*Ja.*" When he continued to stare at her, she turned away to hide her heated cheeks. "I plan to make whoopie pies next."

"I won't keep you long. Mam is finishing the list of people she wants to invite to the reunion. I was wondering if we could set up a time and place to meet during the week."

"The restaurant is open from seven thirty in the morning until three thirty in the afternoon Monday through Friday. Can you meet me there on Monday around four?"

"I'll be there." David headed toward the door and then paused to glance back. "Any chance I can buy one of your desserts to enjoy while we work?" He grinned like a small boy. "Consider it a taste test for the party."

Fannie laughed. "I'll see what I can come up with."

"I have a thought," he said, his blue eyes brightening. "If you'd like to see the list before we get started on Monday, feel free to stop by when you're done cooking for the day."

Given their past and her unresolved feelings toward him, she wasn't sure she should. But they would be working together so it shouldn't feel awkward to pick up the list. If she had it in her possession, she could get an idea of how many people she might need to supply food for. "I will if I have the time. If I don't see you later today, I'll see you tomorrow."

He nodded and left. Fannie felt the tension in her shoulders ease. Sometimes she felt comfortable with him, but the thought of going to his house where she'd be surrounded by his family made her hesitate.

"Did you stop by Fannie's *haus*?" His mother met him at the door when he got home.

David nodded. "We're going to start on the invitations Monday afternoon." He studied her through shrewd eyes. "You do have the invitation list done, *ja*?"

"I do." Concern filled her expression as she examined him. "Are you feeling *oll recht*?"

"I'm fine, Mam." He saw the coffeepot on the stove and went to get a cup.

"Please sit down and spend a few moments with me."

She nodded and sat across from him with her coffee.

"Fannie might stop by to take a look at the list," he told her. "This way she'll get an inkling of how many people she'll need to provide food for."

"That's a *gut* idea." His mother smiled. She narrowed her eyes as she studied him. "Fannie is a lovely young woman."

"She seems nice," he said. *And pretty, too.* "I don't know her well." And he didn't want his mother to realize how much Fannie was in his thoughts since he'd first met her at the luncheonette. And she knew how to take care of his headaches. It wasn't only her hot compresses that had helped him. Fannie's soothing touch on his skin as she changed the compresses had made him better quickly. He took a sip from his coffee cup. "I'm not sure of Fannie's visit this afternoon. She might have too much to do to prepare food for tomorrow's visit to the Gabriel Fishers."

"We'll see her tomorrow," his *mam* said. "We'll bring the list with us to give to her then."

A knock resounded on the outside kitchen entrance as David got settled with a second cup of coffee while his *mam* ran her laundry basket upstairs. He rose and answered the door.

"*Hallo*, David." Fannie offered him a shy smile. "I made it, but I can only stay for a short while."

He returned her smile. "I'm glad you were able to get away." He opened the door wider and held it for her to enter.

His mother entered the room. "Fannie! How lovely to see you." She gestured toward a kitchen chair. "Have a seat. Coffee? Or tea?"

Fannie nodded. "If you have enough, I'd love a coffee."

David watched his mother pour Fannie's drink and set it on the table with cream and sugar. She then pulled a tin of home-made cookies from the pantry. He leaned toward Fannie and whispered, "I hope you like chocolate chip cookies. Mam is going to insist you have at least one."

"What did you say, *soohn*?" his *mam* said as she placed the cookies on the table.

"I told her that you would expect her to have one cookie if not more." David eyed his mother with amusement. He chuckled when she frowned at him. "I'm sure she'll love your cookies, Mam." He flashed Fannie a pleading look.

He saw Fannie's lips twitch. "I'd love to have a couple," she said. *"Danki."*

David grinned, grateful that she'd read his expression correctly.

Mam gave them each a dessert plate before she passed around the tin of cookies. David was overly conscious of Fannie beside him. She had changed her garments since he'd seen her last, and she looked beautiful in her light purple tab dress. He watched as the young woman fixed her coffee the way she liked it before she took two cookies from the tin.

"*Ach*, cookies!" his younger brother exclaimed as he entered the room and then sat down directly across from Fannie. His mother raised an eyebrow when Simeon grabbed a handful of the treats. The teenager grinned as he took a bite of one. "You know I love your cookies, Mam. I always take more than one. I can't help myself." He ate his first treat so fast it was as if he'd inhaled it before he started on another one.

His mother handed her youngest a coffee mug. "It looks like you took four or five, youngest *soohn*."

Simeon's scowl at the endearment quickly became a grin. "Mam, I eat a lot because I'm still a growing boy."

Fannie chuckled at his brother's comment, and the sound made David smile.

The four of them enjoyed their coffee and cookies while they talked about the weather. Fannie asked about his grandparents, and his mother explained that Samuel had taken them for a buggy ride to get them out of the house for a bit. David watched the animation on Fannie's face as they discussed her father's dairy farm. And then the upcoming reunion became the main topic of conversation.

"Joanna, David said the invitation list is ready." Fannie nibbled on another cookie.

"It is." She rose and took a pad of paper from a kitchen drawer. "I believe this is everyone we want to invite. My husband and I went over it carefully and Samuel agrees." His *mam* handed it to Fannie.

Fannie looked over the paper. "Do you mind if I take this home with me? I'll return it to David when we meet Monday afternoon."

Mam looked pleased. "Of course, you may take it home."

"I know we have time before we plan the menu," Fannie said, "but it will be helpful to take a *gut* look at the guest list before I give it back."

"Keep it," his mother said. "I made a duplicate."

"If Mam decides to add anyone else," David said, "I'll let you know." He grinned at his mother. "We may want to add some extra food portions in case my parents decide to invite anyone else at the last minute. And, Mam?"

"Ja, soohn?" His mother eyed him with affection.

"Can we make Monday the last day for changes?" he teased.

His mother gazed at him innocently. "Maybe."

David shook his head and met Fannie's gaze. "See how she is? You've been warned."

Fannie smirked at him. "I'm sure everything will be fine." She rose and collected their cups.

"Fannie, I'll take care of those." Instinctively recognizing her intentions, David stood and took the cups from her. "I know you need to get home, and believe it or not, I've done dishes before."

Simeon laughed. "Sure you have, Bruder."

"He has, Simeon," Mam said quickly. "Perhaps you would like to learn how."

David placed the cups into the sink basin and then filled it with soapy water. With a wave of his hand, he invited his brother to step in and do the job.

The wide-eyed, horrified look on his younger brother's face had them laughing. All except Simeon. His mother raised her eyebrows, and with an exaggerated sigh, the boy rose and went to the sink to wash four coffee cups.

Fannie picked up the pad of paper from the table. "I'll take the pages and leave you the pad."

Mam shook her head. "Keep it. You and David may need it later."

David walked Fannie to her buggy. "I'll see you again soon," he said. There was something about her that continually drew his attention, and he couldn't figure out why.

She nodded. "*Danki* for this," she said as she held up the list.

"I wasn't teasing when I suggested we need to plan for extra people when figuring out how much food to make. Mam said the list is complete, but knowing my *mudder*, it's likely she'll think of someone else to invite as we get closer to the reunion."

Fannie chuckled. "I know. I've been warned."

Chapter Six

It was a beautiful summer day for visiting. A light breeze rustled the leaves on the oak tree that sat in the Gabriel Fishers' backyard. Tables and benches were set up outside so that those who would be visiting could enjoy the gorgeous weather. Fannie had arrived a few moments ago with her father and Alta. After a glance at the number of tables, she carried a macaroni salad and her whoopie pies to the house while Alta followed with three dozen cupcakes. Her father held on to the container of brownies that she'd decided to make at the last minute yesterday afternoon, after she'd gotten home from David's house. She'd left the cake she baked at home for her family's enjoyment throughout the week.

"*Gut mariga*, Lucy." Fannie greeted Gabriel Fisher's wife with a smile.

Lucy grinned. "I'm glad you could come." She caught sight of Alta behind her. "Alta and Jonas, it's *wunderbor* to see you!"

Fannie set the macaroni salad and whoopie pies on the counter and then reached for Alta's cupcakes. Her father, who had entered behind her, handed their hostess the brownies.

Lucy smiled. "Gabriel is in the barn, Jonas. Would you like coffee or tea to take with you?"

"*Nay*, I'm still full from breakfast." Her *dat* offered a smile of thanks. "I'll be in the barn with Gabriel."

It was ten in the morning and the midday meal would be shared at noon. She faced Lucy and Alta, leaning back against the counter.

Lucy reached for the kettle on the stove. "The water's already hot if you want tea. And the coffee's done if you prefer that."

"I'd love a tea." Fannie, being a good friend of Lucy's, knew where everything in her kitchen was stored. She reached up to get cups from a kitchen cabinet. "Alta?"

"*Ja*, tea sounds *gut*." Alta smiled. "Lucy, how are your young ones?"

"Fine. *Wunderbor*. It's hard to believe how fast they are growing. Susan is nearly seven, and Jacob—he'll be four on his next birthday. And our Grace? She's no longer a baby. It seems like yesterday that I held her as a newborn. Now she's walking and toddling after her brother."

"They grow up so quickly," Alta said with a look of sadness.

"Isn't Mary's baby due soon?" Fannie asked.

Alta nodded as she accepted tea bags

from Lucy and placed one in each cup. "*Ja*, any day now."

"You'll be going to New Holland as soon as she has the *bubbel*?" Lucy asked. Mary Hershberger Bontrager, Alta's eldest daughter, lived there with her husband, Ethan.

"I will. I can't help but feel nervous for her, but she has been doing well so far. I probably shouldn't worry so much." Alta sat at the table and watched Fannie pour water into the cups.

Lucy took the seat perpendicular to Alta and smiled at Fannie, who slid a steaming mug in her direction. "You're her *mudder*. Of course, you worry about her."

"*Ja*, Alta. I think you're too hard on yourself." Fannie placed the sugar bowl and a pitcher of milk on the table then took the seat across from her stepmother. "You're a *gut mam*. I hope you realize that I feel as if you're my *mudder* now. You've made my *vadder* extremely happy, and you have been kind and patient with me."

Alta looked at her with tears in her eyes. "Fannie, you're the one who's been kind and patient. And *danki* for that."

While she knew that Alta was sincere, Fannie still thought that she should move out of the house and give her father and Alta their privacy. Living on her own in an apartment would be unconventional within her Amish community, but she wouldn't allow it to deter her from moving there. Since she had no intention of marrying, she knew she could make it happen. She couldn't live in her father's house forever.

"Grab that plastic container, will you?" Lucy asked Fannie. She was closest to where it sat at the other end of the table. "I feel like a cinnamon roll, don't you?"

Fannie knew that Lucy was a master baker who made the best cinnamon rolls. It was because of Lucy's generosity that Fannie had her recipe to use in her restaurant.

The tantalizing scent of cinnamon reached

Fannie's nose as Lucy opened the container then extended it to Alta and then Fannie. Lucy picked one for herself, and they each took a bite and hummed happily at how delicious it was. "I don't think mine come out as good as yours," Fannie said before she took another taste.

"I enjoyed yours the last time Gabriel and I took our family to eat breakfast at your luncheonette, and we loved them." Lucy sipped her tea. "Jacob wanted another, but I didn't think it wise to have that much sugar. He needed a nap when we got back to the *haus*." She took another bite. "Your cinnamon buns taste exactly like mine. I don't make them often for us at home since they sell well in Kings General Store and Peter's Pockets. I bake them occasionally, but you would have thought that our *kinner* had never had them before after they ate one of yours." She laughed. "It's *wunderbor* to enjoy cooking that I don't have to do."

"Where are your little ones?" Alta asked.

"They're with their *vadder*. Gabriel is a fine *dat*. He's made them all special toys." Lucy's eyes widened. "Oops, I forgot to tell Jonas that Gabriel has our *kinner* with him."

"Not to worry," Alta said. "My husband loves them. Unfortunately, he hasn't been able to spend time with his *kins kinner*."

"*Ja*, my older *bruder* and *schweschter* with their families live far from here," Fannie added. "The last time we saw them was five and a half years ago at the funeral." Fannie knew the women were aware that the funeral had been her mother's. She still felt sad whenever she thought of the loss of her *mam*.

The windows were open to allow in the summer breeze. The sound of buggy wheels on the driveway carried loudly into the kitchen.

Lucy stood and closed the lid on the cinnamon roll container. "Looks like the others are starting to arrive."

Fannie picked up their empty teacups

and placed them in the dish basin. She did a quick rinse in sudsy water and then left them. Lucy would finish the job tomorrow morning when it wasn't a Sunday, since no work was allowed today except for the necessary care of animals. She would have come back herself to help Lucy but she had her luncheonette to open first thing.

Fannie went to the window as Lucy and Alta headed outside. She saw Alta's sister Lovina with her husband and five children, followed by Jed and Rachel King and their brood. A third buggy entered the driveway, and she immediately recognized the Troyer family with Samuel and Joanna seated in the front while Simeon, Mary and David were in the back. Her gaze zeroed in on David. Fannie found that she couldn't look away, even if she wanted to.

David didn't feel like being here, but he didn't want to worry or disappoint his parents. His *mam* seemed so excited to see her friends. He didn't know these people, although he'd met Gabriel and Lucy Fisher briefly at church service last Sunday. He climbed out of his family's buggy and waited to see where everyone would go. His mother and sister headed toward the house and his father went to the barn. David hung back with his younger brother.

A young man headed in their direction, and David shot Simeon a questioning glance. *Henry King*, his brother mouthed. Unfortunately, David didn't remember him.

Henry walked up to him. "David, it's *gut* to see you. I saw you during service last week, but I didn't get a chance to talk with you that day."

"Henry," he greeted. "I'm sorry. I've been away so long, I have trouble putting names to faces."

"Then let me introduce myself," Henry said. "I'm Henry King, and I'm the oldest of five. My *eldre* are Adam and Lovina

King. I have two *bruders*, Isaiah and Jebidiah, and two *schweschters*, Linda and Esther."

David narrowed his gaze thoughtfully. "Linda...does she work at Fannie's Luncheonette?"

"*Ja*, she does." Henry smiled. "Esther helps out on occasion when she's not cleaning houses."

"Do you know my *bruder*, Simeon?" David glanced at his sibling.

"Simeon." Henry nodded. "Do you know mine? Isaiah just turned thirteen. Jebidiah is the youngest at eleven."

Simeon shook his head. "I'm seventeen." He glanced across the yard toward some other boys. "Do they like baseball?"

"*Ja*, as do I." After waving his brothers over, Henry faced Simeon. "Maybe we can play later."

"Sounds *gut*," Simeon said.

The man eyed him. "David?"

"I don't think so, Henry, but *danki* for asking. I've been having some trouble with headaches, and I'd rather not do anything to bring one on again."

"I understand." The eldest King sibling clearly did by the look of compassion he offered.

"I can watch, though," David said as Henry's brothers joined them.

While Henry invited his siblings to play a game of baseball later, David found his gaze wandering toward the house where Fannie exited with two other women, all three carrying dishes.

David heard her laugh out loud and watched her interact with those around her. It was obvious that those in her group liked her. His brother was talking with the King brothers, but David didn't hear a word. He was too focused on the woman across the yard from him. Her blond hair looked golden in the sunlight. Her dress was pale blue, which he knew would highlight her blue eyes. Fannie set down a platter then headed back to the house, and he looked away. He had no right to stare. She could never be in his life, even if she did come to like him. His mind constantly fought to find his memories—to place faces like Henry King's—and the woman didn't know him well enough to know if she liked him or not.

"David." His brother's voice brought him back to the conversation in his group. "You sure you don't want to play baseball?"

"I don't think it's a *gut* idea, Simeon. But you go ahead, and I'll watch from the sidelines. *Okey?*" David smiled at his brother and the others.

"Sounds fine to me," Henry said. "Do you think you can make calls like an umpire for us?"

He frowned. "Make calls?"

Henry nodded. "*Ja*, outs and strikes. That kind of thing."

David hesitated. "I don't know." He didn't think it would be wise under the circumstances. Not with his headaches that often came too fast to predict. Besides, he only vaguely recalled the game of baseball and worried that everyone would know. It was better if he watched the game from a distance, then baseball and its rules might come back to him.

"I'll play, cousin," a newcomer said as he joined the group.

"Wunderbor!" Henry grinned. "Have you met our cousin Thomas King? His parents are Jed and Rachel. Do you remember meeting them? Jed is my *dat*'s *bruder.*"

He frowned as he fought to remember. "Do they run the general store?"

"*Ja.* Jed's parents own the store, but they've stepped away from it. Jed will get it eventually anyway."

Henry turned to his cousin. "Where's Moses? He's going to play ball later, *recht*?"

Thomas smiled. "*Ja.* I'll let him know we'll be playing after lunch." Then he walked away.

Fannie exited the house with a huge bowl. David watched her cross the yard and set it on the food table with the other dishes. His mother approached her and said something that made her grin. Something inside of him hurt as he watched them. He closed his eyes and fought hard to remember. Until he recovered, he could never have anyone in his life, especially someone like Fannie.

The others walked away, leaving David standing alone. He took a seat at one of the tables and continued to observe as women carried items out of the house for the midday meal. David stood abruptly when it occurred to him that he could help. Starting toward the house, he stopped when Fannie came outside again.

"May I take that from you?" he asked.

She appeared surprised. "Sure."

"I'd like to help," he told her. "May I?"

When he nodded, she said, "Ah, sure." And she handed over a plate of cold roast beef.

David smiled at her and then walked to the food table to find a place for it. He saw a platter of ham and placed the roast beef next to it within easy reach. When he turned to head toward the house, he saw that Fannie hadn't left. She stood near the steps, watching him.

He approached and stopped in front of her. "What else can I do?"

"David—"

"Honestly, I want to help."

"You don't need to do anything." Fannie couldn't keep her eyes off him. "Everything is here except for the desserts, and I'll bring those out later." She'd loved him once, and now she continued to worry about him after seeing him suffer a debilitating headache last week.

"Fannie, I *like* to help." He glanced toward the location in question. "It looks like there is already a second table there for desserts. Please let me carry out the desserts with you."

Looking into his gorgeous blue eyes, Fannie melted. *"Oll recht."*

The door opened as David followed her up the stairs. Joanna Troyer held a dish.

She smiled at Fannie and caught sight of her son. "David!"

"Just coming inside to pick up desserts," he told her.

"You've always been ready to lend a hand," she said softly with a look of affection.

David's *mam* went directly to the main food table and set down her bowl. Fannie recognized it as one holding sweet and sour chow-chow, a delicious blend of pickled garden vegetables that had been left at the end of last year's growing season.

Fannie nodded at David, then climbed the steps and went inside as Lucy Fisher held the door open for her and David.

"*Danki*, Lucy. David is going to carry out desserts with me." Fannie reached for Alta's containers and handed them to him. "There are three dozen cupcakes. Should be plenty with everything else we have."

His eyes were on her lips when he nodded. Fannie felt her face heat, and she quickly turned to grab two cakes and preceded him out of the house. She sensed him directly behind her and headed toward the dessert table. After placing the two cakes, she watched him carefully set down the cupcakes. David straightened and met her gaze. "Are any of the desserts yours?"

Fannie nodded. "The brownies inside the *haus*. I believe Lucy baked the cherry and apple pies. I made the whoopie pies, which are my *vadder*'s favorite."

They walked toward the house. "Your *dat* is a kind man."

"*Ja*, he is. He's always been, even before my *mudder*…" Her voice trailed off. She didn't like talking about her late mother. Lena Miller had been a wonderful parent and wife, and Fannie still felt the loss although it had gotten a little easier to cope with over the years. Alta was wonderful, and Fannie was grateful to have her stepmother in her life. It had helped to ease some of the pain she'd suffered since her mother's death. She loved Alta and thought the woman was perfect for her father.

"What about your *mudder*?" David studied her with curiosity. "She seems nice. She made the cupcakes, *ja*?"

Fannie smiled. "Alta is my stepmother, and I love her. But I was talking about my *mam* who passed on over five years ago." It had been a stormy night when her mother had collapsed, which only worsened her fear of thunderstorms that had started at an early age. One minute her mother had been there and in the next she was gone. Fannie recalled the violence of the storm as they waited for the ambulance. By the time it arrived, Mam was gone.

David blinked and grew quiet. He wore a thoughtful look. "I'm sorry. That must have been before we left New Berne. Did I know her?"

"*Nay.*" Fannie started back to the house with David beside her. "Your family became members of our church district after the bishop split up your old one because the congregation had become too big. I was sixteen when she died. You joined our community over a year later."

"So, I never met her." He reached for the screen door, which he held open for her.

"Not unless you happened to encounter her in Kings General Store. Mam didn't get out of the *haus* much. She preferred being at home. My sister, Sadie, did the shopping and ran errands for her until she married and moved away. And then I did what I could to help out." Fannie had never understood why her mother had a problem interacting with others. Her *mam* had attended church service with the family, and although she chatted with some of the women, she often left any groups to seek a moment alone.

Once inside the house, David waited for her instructions. "You can take the brownies," Fannie said, "since I made so many, while I get the two pies."

It wasn't long after she and David had brought out the last of the desserts, including her whoopie pies, when Gabriel Fisher announced that lunch was ready.

Everyone went to get food. The Troyers sat with the Fishers at one table, and the Adam Kings sat with Fannie, Alta and Fannie's father. Adam's brother Jed and his family sat with Fannie's brothers DJ and Danny who'd arrived only a short time ago. Fannie could hear her brothers laughing with Jed's sons.

The meal was delicious, and Fannie hoped everyone enjoyed her macaroni salad and desserts. As she ate her lunch, she reflected on the warmth she'd felt by her chat with David earlier, and his thoughtful offer to help... She shook her head and focused on Alta's conversation with her sister, forcing David from her mind. It was for the best. Her future lay with her luncheonette, not with David Troyer.

Chapter Seven

After a pleasant meal talking with the people at her table, Fannie sat back and watched with a smile as friends and family rose and headed to the dessert table. The sun was high in the sky, and the temperature was warm. It was late June, and she wasn't surprised by how nice it was. She caught sight of her father and Alta getting dessert. Alta's nephew Isaiah said something to her as he grabbed two cupcakes. Her father's wife laughed, clearly delighted in whatever the boy had to say. When she saw Isaiah bite enthusiastically into a cupcake as he made his way back to his table, Fannie knew. The thirteen-year-old loved Alta's treats.

A glance back at her parents made Fannie grin. The love between them was easily seen. Her *dat* teased his wife as he grabbed a taste of everything except her cupcakes. When Alta pretended to pout, Fannie's father laughed and reached around her for a cupcake. Moments later, they walked back to their table where Fannie sat.

"Finally took one of her cupcakes, Dat?" Fannie laughed at the look on her father's face. She loved how playful and affectionate they were with each other.

"*Ja*, she made me." He looked downtrodden as he set his plate on the table and sat down.

"I made you!" Alta let out a humph that quickly turned to laughter after Jonas stared at her and then leaned closer to kiss her cheek. "Fannie, you'd best get some dessert before it's all gone."

"I'm not sure I need any." But Fannie stood to go. She had listened to her parents with longing for a love like theirs, something she could have had with David if life had taken a different turn. A sudden awareness of someone's gaze on her had her glancing toward the Troyers to encounter David. A small smile curved his masculine lips. She quickly looked away and then went to get a treat. David's smile, those blue eyes...

She recalled the first time she'd met him. She'd been seventeen and his family recently had been moved into her church district. She'd liked everything about him, and they'd become fast friends. Then when she'd turned nineteen and he was twenty-one, he'd told her he wanted to spend more time with her. They'd shared picnics and gone on walks. David had taken her home from a singing one time, but then they'd reached a point when they hadn't felt the need to attend. They'd only wanted to be together. Fannie sighed. She'd had high hopes of being his wife. She could have had a life with him, been the mother to his children. It hurt too much to think about what could have been.

Forcing the thought from her mind, she checked out the desserts and decided on a slice of Lucy's apple pie and one of Alta's cupcakes. She turned to go back... and found the man of her thoughts heading toward her.

David made his way over to the dessert table. Glancing at Fannie, he allowed his gaze to collide with hers briefly before he nodded and looked away. He reached for a brownie and enjoyed its rich chocolate flavor. He knew Fannie had made them. He wanted to try one of her whoopie pies next and moved down the table as Fannie returned to her seat.

David didn't mind planning the reunion with her. He enjoyed spending time with her, although he probably shouldn't. The only thing that bothered him was his parents' reason for hosting a reunion in the first place. He felt overwhelmed by the knowledge that they would be inviting a bunch of people he probably didn't know. Didn't his family understand that he had trouble with large groups of people? The number of people here on the Fishers' property made him uncomfortable. He was happy to sit at a table with his family and the Fishers. They were nice people, and their youngsters were well-behaved. But the thought of having to stand amid a gathering of people he didn't know—family members he wouldn't remember—unnerved him. Had he always been this way? Or were these feelings a symptom of his amnesia?

Henry came over. "We're getting ready to play baseball now. You going to watch us?"

David headed to the open space in the yard where Henry's brother Isaiah had made bases from flat rocks and sticks. He looked around for a chair and saw one close to the house. Grabbing its back, he repositioned the chair so he could see the makeshift baseball field.

The game started with four on each team. David met Fannie's twin brothers who were picked to be on Thomas and Moses King's team. Henry, Isaiah and Jebidiah would play with Simeon. As he waited for the game to start, David felt a sudden presence as someone moved a chair next to his and sat down. He was stunned to see it was Fannie.

He smiled at her. "Are you a fan of baseball?"

Fannie responded in kind. "Have you met my twin *bruders*? I learned to play when I was ten."

"Fannie," one of the twins called. "You going to play?" They were both dark-haired like their father and had Jonas Miller's warm brown eyes.

"*Nay*, DJ." Fannie grinned. "I'll watch."

"David." Simeon drew his attention. "Are you going to stand behind home plate and umpire or not?"

"Not," he said with a smirk. "Since when do you need an umpire anyway?"

To his surprise, Fannie stood. "I'll do it."

"Ach nay!" her brother Danny said. "You're biased!"

"How is that?" Ignoring his complaints, Fannie took a position behind home plate.

"You like the King *bruders* better than your own." The amused look in the man's expression confirmed that he was teasing his sister.

"With *gut* reason!" she quipped, her face brimming with laughter.

David watched the game, enthralled as Fannie made calls and put players in their places when they gave her a hard time. He could tell that she was enjoying herself. Fannie had a close relationship with her siblings, and he could see that she liked spending time with them. The game went on for about two hours before the players called it quits. His father and Fannie's father helped Gabriel break down the makeshift tables and put away the benches.

Fannie passed him as she headed toward the house. He had loved watching the game, observing her. She seemed so familiar now to him. Was it because of the number of times he'd seen her?

"You were a *wunderbor* umpire," he commented as he fell into step beside her.

She paused and looked at him. *"Danki."*

"Loved the way you kept all the players in line," David said. "I can tell that you get along well with your *bruders*."

"Experience." She flashed him a grin and then continued toward the house. Fannie halted at the bottom of the stoop and faced him. "We're still meeting at four tomorrow, *ja*?"

"I'll be there," he assured her before she went into the house.

David put back his chair and the one that Fannie barely used. Visiting Day had turned out much better than he'd thought. He'd had a good time and remained headache free. Catching sight of his *dat*, he went to help clean up the yard. Despite the problems he faced each day because of his amnesia, he realized that he was blessed to have a family like his and to live in a community where everyone was open, friendly and there for each other.

Fannie couldn't stop thinking about Visiting Day when David had praised her abilities as an umpire. When she'd brought a chair over to sit with him, he'd seemed surprised but pleased to see her. When she'd jumped up to be an umpire for the baseball game, David looked stunned. A small smile played about her lips as she recalled how amused he'd been at the exchange between her and her brothers… and how she'd refused to allow the players to give her a hard time.

Fannie drove her pony cart into the lot behind her restaurant the next morning and tied up her horse near the outbuilding where she kept supplies and housed her mare and cart whenever it rained. She unlocked the back door and slipped inside, turning the dead bolt behind her. It was early again at six o'clock. Last night she couldn't sleep as she wondered how she and David would work together to come up with a menu and then write invitations and address the envelopes.

They could discuss this when they met, but she thought that she and David could drop off the invitations to the Troyer family members who lived in Lancaster County in person. The rest they could mail to the people who lived out of state.

The first thing she did was make coffee. She needed a cup to get through the day. While the brew perked, Fannie grabbed paper place mats and silverware to prepare the tables in the dining room. Working from the front toward the back, she placed the table settings after making sure each table was cleaned and disinfected. She did everything automatically, for it was something she often did when she arrived well before the luncheonette opened. A knock on the front window made her jump. After taking deep breaths to slow her heart rate, she turned and saw a familiar face through the glass. *David.*

She opened the door for him. "I thought we weren't meeting until four."

"I know. I couldn't sleep and came out for a walk. Fannie, I didn't expect to see you this morning, but once I did, I knew I needed to talk with you."

Fannie stepped back to allow his entry. "I put coffee on. Would you like a cup?"

David studied her intently a moment before he looked away. *"Ja, danki."*

"Have a seat, and I'll be right back." Surprised, she wondered what he needed to discuss so early in the morning. Fannie poured them each a mug of coffee and then automatically fixed his coffee with cream and sugar the way he liked it, the way she remembered from over two years ago now. She set a cup down before him carefully then sat across from him.

David looked down into his coffee before he took a sip. His eyes widened as he met her gaze. "You know how I take my coffee?"

Fannie shrugged. "I fixed it the way I like it." *The way we both like it.*

He took another drink. "It's perfect. *Danki.*"

"So, what would you like to talk about?" she asked after a moment of silence.

He looked uncomfortable and delayed having a conversation with a sip from his coffee. David set down his cup and his blue eyes captured hers. "I need to know. Did my *eldre* force you to agree to work with me? I understand that you want to cater the reunion, but it seemed that you are going above and beyond in helping with this event."

She paused a moment to choose her words carefully. As she thought about it, Fannie realized that she wanted to work with David. Knowing how hard it was for him since he'd lost his memory due to some vicious attack made her want to do everything she could to help him.

"David, I thought we'd talked about this. I'm happy to help. Your parents didn't force me to accept anything. I am pleased to cater your family reunion, and I confess that, at first, I was surprised when Joanna and Samuel asked me to plan it with you. But I'm happy to help. *Oll recht?* Don't worry about it. I know this can't be easy for you—"

He sighed. "It's not. The thought of spending time with people I don't know who are supposedly related to me scares me." The words seemed to tumble out.

Fannie reached out to place her hand over his. "I'll be there, and you know me. And we'll get the chance to know each other better while we work together." She saw his surprise and felt his shock as he stared at her hand on top of his. Embarrassed, she quickly withdrew her touch. "Sorry."

David looked up and connected with her through his blue gaze. "Why?"

She felt her face heat. "I overstepped."

He smiled. "*Nay.* You made me feel better."

His genuine gratitude made her smile... until she remembered that this was her first catering job. She couldn't fail David's parents and family. An event like this one could make or break the future of her catering business and she needed to focus.

"I looked over the list," she said. "We're inviting fifty-five people. But fifteen invitations, one for each family, should be enough."

"What will we do for invitations?"

She rose. "We can shop together and look at what's available."

David nodded. Then he reached into his pocket and pulled out some dollar bills.

"Don't even think about paying for the coffee. The restaurant isn't open yet. The coffee came from a friend, not a luncheonette owner."

He gave her a soft smile. "But you returned my ten dollars after you found it. Please let me pay this time."

"*Nay*, David. We are working together. The coffee is on me."

"*Danki*, Fannie."

She felt a flutter in her stomach, as the way he looked at her was familiar. Warm. The same way he'd gazed at her when they were younger.

David went to the front door. "Don't forget to lock the door behind me. I wouldn't want someone to stumble inside uninvited." He grinned. "Have a *wunderbor* day. I'll see you later."

"The same to you." She followed him to the door, and after he left, she locked it. "See you at four."

Fannie stood a moment in the dining room, lost in the past. Then she glanced at the wall clock and went to work. She had too much to do to dawdle.

Chapter Eight

That afternoon at three, Fannie and Linda wiped down the tables and prepared them for their customers the next day. There were no diners in her eatery, and when it was this late, Fannie closed the luncheonette.

Linda went into the kitchen and returned moments later with place settings. Once the tables were ready, Fannie entered the kitchen and turned on the dishwasher. With the low hum of the machine as background noise, she moved packages of ground beef and pork chops from the freezer to the refrigerator. She'd offer hamburgers and stuffed pork chops as the specials tomorrow. There were always sandwiches and other items on the menu; she liked to give her customers a choice between a light lunch or a full meal with sides.

At Fannie's insistence earlier, Linda had set aside a generous helping of today's chicken noodle casserole special to take home to her family. "I'll see you tomorrow morning, Fannie."

"*Ja*, see you then, Linda."

Her employee started to leave before the young woman halted and turned. "I spoke with my aunt Rachel recently. She said that Hannah Lapp, one of her cousins from Happiness, is coming for a visit. The young woman will be in New Berne for an extended stay. She thinks Hannah would enjoy working here rather than at Kings General Store. I'll find out when she's due to arrive and get more information to see if she is interested in working here."

Fannie grinned. "Sounds *gut*. Do you know how long she'll be staying?" The only downside was if Hannah was only here for a few weeks.

"I'm not sure, but Aunt Rachel made it sound as if she planned to stay the summer and into the fall." Linda smiled. "I'll leave you to it. I don't know what you have left to do, but don't work too hard."

"*Gut nacht*, Linda. Tell your family *hallo* for me."

"Will do." Linda left, leaving Fannie alone in the building with only the drone of the dishwasher. She went into the dining room to clear a table for her meeting with David at four.

With thoughts of her current living situation and the time to spare before David's arrival, Fannie climbed the steps to the second floor and studied the large open space. It would take work, but she was sure the area could be converted into an apartment. Her main worry was that her father might be upset with the idea of her living alone. But it felt right for her to move so that her *dat* and Alta would enjoy the privacy they deserved as newlyweds. As for the church elders' opinions... Her *dat* was one of them and if he accepted it, then they would also. But first, he had to approve of her decision to move out.

Surveying the area, she envisioned where she could put a bathroom with a shower and a small kitchen cabinet unit with a sink and countertop. A stove wouldn't be necessary, for she could cook on the one in her luncheonette's commercial kitchen. And she could take what was left of her restaurant's special for the day and heat it downstairs. Not only would she be out of her father's house, but it would be convenient to live upstairs from her place of business. The first step would be to get a price on installing a bathroom with a shower. She pulled her cell phone out of her apron waistband and dialed Jed King at Kings General Store. Jed used to work in construction and would have the information she would need. When he answered after two rings, Fannie smiled.

"Jed, it's Fannie Miller. Do you know a *gut* plumber? I need some work done at the restaurant."

He asked her to hold on and then returned to the phone with a name—Robert Steele—and his phone number.

"*Danki*, Jed."

"You're *willkomm*, Fannie," Jed said. "Robert is a *gut* man. You can trust him. Let me know if I can help in any way."

Fannie thanked him again and then called Robert. During the call, she asked him if he could come to the luncheonette to give her an estimate for installing a full bathroom upstairs. Fortunately for her, Robert Steele not only came highly recommended as a plumber but also as a contractor. Robert had a free moment this coming Saturday at eight thirty in the morning.

By the time she had ended the call, Fannie was thrilled. The prospect of moving excited her. It would be an adventure to live here, although she would miss seeing her father and Alta daily. But she would still bring them food and spend time with them then, and she hoped they would come to the luncheonette for meals. There was only one thing she dreaded, and it was having to tell her *dat* of her plans.

Fannie heard noise from the first floor near the rear entrance door. Starting down the stairs, she called out, "Linda, what did you forget?" When she reached the bottom, she saw it was David, not her friend.

"I'm sorry," he said. "It's just me." He shifted awkwardly as if he knew he'd overstepped. "I'm a little early. I knocked but there was no answer, so I came inside to look for you."

She smiled. "That's fine. Come in. I cleared a table for us in the dining room."

David had changed clothes since this morning. He looked good in a light blue short-sleeved shirt and navy tri-blend pants with navy suspenders. "Are you ready to get to work?" he asked.

Fannie caught sight of the paper he held. "What's that?" she asked as she pulled out two chairs for them to sit.

"As expected, Mam added another family to the list." With a shake of his head, he handed it to her. "If everyone attends, you'll have sixty people to feed."

Fannie looked over the names and addresses of the added invitees, then wrote their names and information on the original list with the others.

"I don't understand why Mam feels the need to invite so many." David sounded frustrated. "I don't know anyone."

"I'm sorry, David." She eyed him with compassion. "This must be hard for you."

He nodded. "I'm not looking forward to it." David shrugged. "There is nothing else to do but go along with my parents' wishes." He sat in his chair. "My *mudder* wants us to make the final decision about the menu," he said quietly.

"*Gut* to know." She took the seat across from him.

"I believe our first order of business is the invitations." He seemed overwhelmed by the event and the work necessary for it to be successful.

He rubbed his clean-shaven jaw and appeared thoughtful. "I say we shop for them. It's quicker and easier."

"Did your *mudder* or *vadder* give you a budget?" Fannie asked.

He shook his head. "*Nay*, but I'm not worried about the cost. Let's sort that today and we can discuss food at our next meeting."

"Do you have a job schedule we need to work around?" Fannie wondered if he was currently employed or if he was free to meet and deliver the invitations whenever she was available. Some part of her hoped to hear that he'd gotten back his apprenticeship with Amos Mast at Mast Furniture Shop.

"*Nay*, no work yet, although I'm looking for it." David leaned back in his chair.

"Do you know what you'd like to do?"

He shook his head. "I must have had a job in the past, but I can't remember what I did or if I have any skills."

"Didn't you once work for a cabinet-maker?" Fannie studied him intently and saw the surprise in his blue eyes. "I remember someone mentioned it when you lived here last."

"I did?" He appeared stunned by her question. "I honestly don't remember." The last was said in a whisper.

She hated to see him suffer. "Maybe your *dat* can shed some light on it."

Fannie saw him bite the inside of his cheek. "Why not ask him, David? He might be able to help you. You'll be no worse if your *vadder* doesn't know." She wondered why his family hadn't suggested Amos Mast as a potential employer. Unless his parents didn't want him to work because they would worry too much about him with his amnesia. She felt it best to change the subject. "Would you like an iced tea?"

"Sure." His blue eyes suddenly twinkled as he looked at her. "And a snack?"

She laughed. "Chocolate, lemon or vanilla?"

"You have chocolate cake?" He appeared pleased by the prospect.

"I do." Fannie stood. "I'll be right back." In the kitchen, she poured out glasses of iced tea and pulled two plates of chocolate cake from the dessert refrigeration unit.

"Looks delicious," David said as she returned and set the chocolate cake with his cold tea on the table. "If we use store-bought invitations, it will save us time and we can buy more if we need them." He took a bite of the chocolate treat. "This is *gut* cake." His warm gaze signaled his pleasure.

"I'm glad you like it." She drank from her iced tea before she picked up her fork to eat. Fannie spread out the full list in the middle of the table where they both could examine it. "We have time to purchase invitations this afternoon."

"Okey." David ate another forkful of moist chocolate. "Let's finish our snack and then we can go."

It was raining a short time later when he and Fannie hurried into his buggy and then headed toward the store. David flipped a switch to turn on the battery-operated windshield wipers before he grabbed the leathers and turned the buggy in the lot. "Where to?" he asked. With a flick of the reins, he steered the horse to the edge of the road.

"We could try Kings General Store," Fannie suggested.

He shook his head as he drove his vehicle onto the street. "How about a dollar store?" He could feel her stare before he turned to see it. "What?"

Fannie shook her head. "Nothing." He heard a low humming sound from her as she appeared to give it some thought. "I never considered a dollar store. There is a place called Nick and Nack's Dollar Store. Let's try there. I'm sure we'll find some that are nice and affordable."

Ten minutes later, David wandered through the store with Fannie until they found the card aisle. There were packs of eight one-sided invitations that were a bargain at $1.50. They studied each style carefully until they found the right design, with a green border around the edge and spaces for the reunion information in a white center. He grabbed three packages to make sure they had enough before he took them to the cash register to pay. Smiling, he met Fannie's gaze. "Do you need to buy anything before we leave?"

"Nay." She joined him at the counter. There was a clock on the wall behind the cash register. David saw her glance at it. "It's only four thirty. Do you want to go back to the restaurant and get a head start on these?"

"*Ja*, why not?" He grinned. "The sooner we get them written, the sooner we can start to deliver them." It had stopped raining when they exited the store.

He drove them back to Fannie's Luncheonette, parked his buggy under an overhang in the outbuilding near the back and waited for Fannie to unlock her restaurant. They entered and crossed to the dining room where Fannie pulled out a chair for him at the table closest to the kitchen. David set down their purchase and pulled the invitation packs before he sat.

"Would you like something to drink?" Fannie asked. "Maybe coffee or hot tea?"

To his surprise, the temperature inside felt much cooler than outside. He heard the hum of the air conditioner set for her customers' comfort. The dampness that still clung to his hair and clothes made him chilly.

"Hot tea, please." David smiled. "I'm a

little cold with my wet clothes from the rain."

Fannie nodded. "I could use some to warm me up as well." She left the room for the kitchen.

David waited patiently for her return. So far, he liked working with Fannie. He had a feeling that they could become good friends. Having a friend who accepted him the way he was made him smile. Even if he never regained his memory, he was still grateful for the new caring people in his life. He had plenty of room in his life for them… He could never marry or have a family, though. David had no idea what sort of man he'd been before the incident that had stolen his past. It wouldn't be fair. How could he become involved with a woman, fall in love, when he didn't know himself?

Fannie approached with two mugs of steaming hot tea. She set one before him and then left, returning within seconds with a sugar bowl and a pitcher of cream.

She reached for a pack of invitations and unwrapped it while David did the same. "After we fill these out, we can hand-deliver to those who live close by in New Berne or other parts of Lancaster County," she said while he watched her study the updated list. "It looks like there is only one family who lives some distance away. We can mail theirs."

"Sounds like a fine plan." While David opened the third pack of invitations, Fannie left the room and returned with two black ballpoint pens. She handed him a pen, and then he and Fannie went to work filling in the event's date, time and location on each invitation. His mother had specified the date and time next month, and the reunion would take place at their family home. About a half hour later, they finished.

"When do you want to deliver these?" Fannie's blue gaze was beautiful and curious.

"How about Wednesday afternoon at the

same time?" he said as he stood. "We'll deliver what we can then, which I hope will be all those that don't have to be mailed. If we don't get them done, we'll finish up on Thursday. We can drop off the one invitation we need to mail and then hand-deliver the rest on the other side of town."

"Okey." She rose and picked up their dirty cups. "I feel *gut* about the invitations." She smiled. "They are plain yet pretty."

David grinned at her. "*Ja.* My family will approve."

Fannie walked him to the back door. "I'll see you on Wednesday if not before."

"I'm looking forward to it." He felt his face heat at the admission and quickly added, "It will be *wunderbor* to get these out so there will be one less thing for us to do."

She didn't seem to notice what he'd said. "If it rains, we'll still go. *Ja?*"

She seemed nervous. "*Ja*, unless there is a *gut* reason not to?"

"*Nay*. A little rain is *okey*. I don't care for being on the road during a heavy downpour, though."

"That can be dangerous," David agreed. "We'll pull over if the weather turns bad. *Ja?*" He smiled when she nodded. "Please make a list if you can think of anything we should do next after the invitations are out."

"I will," she said, looking relieved. "Enjoy your night, David."

He reflected on their progress on his drive home. David was surprised how comfortable he felt working with her. No doubt because she was friendly yet professional. He sighed. Someday he would conquer his amnesia. When he did, he would recall how he'd first met her when he joined her church district...and if he'd been as intrigued with her then as he was now.

Chapter Nine

Near the end of Wednesday's workday, Fannie was tired. She hadn't slept well the last two nights after working closely with David Monday afternoon. She couldn't stop thinking about the past when she and David had enjoyed spending time together. *He isn't the same man.* But that didn't make her reaction to him any easier to accept. Yes, she was still attracted to him. And why wouldn't she be? While he didn't remember her, they'd still once shared a past. There was no sense worrying about her reaction to David as long as she kept herself safe from heartbreak. Once was enough to last a lifetime.

David and she were planning a Troyer family event. This was business for her, and she mustn't forget that.

Fannie was in the kitchen when the bells on the front entrance door jingled. "Linda?" she called to her employee who was on the other side of the kitchen. "We have another customer."

"I'll take care of it!" Linda stepped back from the freezer. "I took out cinnamon buns to thaw for tomorrow morning." She smiled as she set them on the ledge close to the dessert case before she headed toward the dining room.

"Linda," Fannie said, stopping her. "I need to hire two more employees now. You've been working long hours and it's not fair to you."

Linda smiled. "I'm fine, but I understand. I checked with Rachel, and her cousin Hannah is interested in working here during her stay."

"Will you ask around to see if anyone

else is looking for work?" Fannie ran the back of her hand across her forehead.

"Will do." She left for the front but came back only seconds later. "It's Mary Troyer. She wants a brief word with you."

Fannie set down her spoon. She'd been making rice pudding. She turned off the heat under the rice and then went to meet Mary in the dining room. "Mary," she greeted with a smile. "This is a pleasant surprise."

"It's nice to see you again," David's sister said. "I've come to apologize. I wanted to help with the invitations, but I have a new job and can't take the time off."

"David and I are doing fine. In fact, we plan to deliver them this afternoon. Congratulations on the job. What are you doing?"

"I've been hired as a receptionist in the new veterinary practice in town. Dr. Zook is young and works with computers." Mary wrinkled her nose as if the idea of working with computers upset her. "He isn't Amish but his family used to be. His parents were Swartzentruber Amish from Ohio. The sect is a lot more conservative than we are."

Fannie nodded. "Do you like your employer?"

Mary shrugged. "I haven't worked with him long. He seems nice enough, but I guess time will tell." She hesitated with a scowl. "And I'll have to learn how to use the computer."

"I'm sure you'll do fine." Fannie smiled. "Would you like coffee or tea? My treat."

"*Nay*, I need to go. I have a few things to pick up for my *mam*." Mary headed to the door where she stopped briefly. "I sincerely hope that our family get-together will help trigger David's memories."

Fannie inclined her head and then watched David's sister leave. She hoped so, too. As she headed back to the kitchen, she thought of David and couldn't imagine how hard it must be for him to have his past wiped out abruptly.

Linda had taken over cooking the rice and was stirring it over the flame when Fannie entered.

By the time she locked up the restaurant, the rice pudding was done and the dishes, bowls and pans were placed in the dishwasher, which she'd turned on.

"I'll see you in the morning," Linda called before she left.

"*Danki* for the good work today." Fannie smiled at her when Linda murmured appreciation then watched as her friend walked out the rear entrance.

A knock thundered the back door.

Fannie hesitated before answering and then smiled when she saw who it was. "David."

"Fannie!" He grinned as he entered. "Ready to make deliveries?"

"*Ja.* Give me a few seconds." She went into the kitchen and picked up the box of invitations with a roll of tape. Fannie walked with David toward his buggy. "All set. Where should we go first?"

"Since we got a later start than I antici-pated, why don't we deliver those who live in New Berne and the area surrounding it?" He opened the buggy door for her. "Then we can branch out into other areas of Lancaster County next time."

"That sounds like a *gut* plan." She set her box on the front seat before she lifted a foot to climb into his vehicle. David hur-ried to assist her. Feeling her face heat, she thanked him without making eye contact and waited for him to get in on the other side.

She picked up the box and set it on her lap. Fannie pushed the roll of tape aside and pulled out a specific stack of invi-tations that had been rubber-banded to-gether by delivery location.

Fannie gave David directions to the ad-dress of the first family on the list. He pulled into the driveway five minutes later, and she handed him the invitation for the address.

"Will you walk up with me?" he asked, appearing uncertain.

"Of course." Fannie understood why he was nervous—he didn't know the people they were inviting. She climbed out before he could assist and then walked beside him to the front door of the house.

David knocked and they waited, then knocked again with no answer. Fannie debated what to do. "Let's tape the invitation to the back door since most families use the rear entrance rather than the front." She faced him. "This way they won't miss it."

His lips curved with good humor. "That's a *wunderbor* idea."

She smiled. "That's why I brought tape. I'll get it and meet you at the back door."

He nodded and started around the house while Fannie went back to his buggy to retrieve the tape.

"We should probably knock one more time before we do this," she said as she reached his side.

David knocked and stepped back. Fannie didn't see a buggy as she searched the barnyard while they waited. "I'll tape this here." She opened the screen door and then stuck the envelope with the family's name on the metal door that led directly into the house's interior.

David drove to another address in his former church district where no one was at home, and he taped the invitation to the door like Fannie did the last time.

At the next location, Fannie knocked, and a young man answered.

"David Troyer! It's *gut* to see you," the man gushed. He introduced himself to Fannie as Lloyd Hostetler before he continued his conversation with David. "When did you get back in town?"

"A few weeks ago," David replied with a small smile. Fannie could see how uncomfortable David was after he was greeted by name, and he had no memory of the person carrying on a conversation with him. "What have you got there?"

"My family is having a reunion of sorts," David said politely. "It's your invitation to the party."

"How are your parents, David?" Lloyd studied him intently.

"They are fine. Thank you for asking. And your family?" He blushed, likely feeling guilty because he didn't know their names. Lloyd continued to talk, and David started looking a bit panicked. Fannie took over the conversation. "I apologize but we have more invitations to deliver today. Will you and your family be able to attend?"

Lloyd said he would check and get back to them. Fannie grabbed David's hand, and he appeared grateful as she tugged him toward his vehicle.

They continued to each address and were able to deliver the invitations quickly before they moved on to the last one.

"I can't believe we delivered the majority of them," David said with a quick smile in her direction before his attention returned to the road.

Fannie returned his smile. "We can finish on Saturday if you'd like. I have a few things to do at the luncheonette first thing. If you come by at eleven, I should be done. And then we can mail the out-of-state invitation as planned before we finish delivering the local ones."

David nodded. *"Oll recht."*

Within minutes, he drove around to the back of her restaurant. He pulled close to the door, parked and got out, lifting a hand to help her.

Unwilling to reject him, she accepted his assistance. "Do you want me to keep the box?"

"Ja. You're organized," he told her. "And I don't want to see it staring me in the face when I'm not sure how I feel about the whole thing."

"Are you *okey*?" she said softly as she gazed up at him. He was so handsome. She'd considered herself a lucky girl when he'd first paid attention to her. The thought of what happened and the loss of something good because of it brought her to tears, which she quickly blinked away.

"I'm fine." He lifted her chin with one finger. "Fannie, what's wrong?"

She released a sharp breath and withdrew before she gave him a genuine smile. He didn't need to know how hurt she'd been after he'd disappeared. And now because he didn't remember her or their past due to his memory loss.

"David, maybe we shouldn't wait until Saturday to get the rest of the invitations out," she said, eager to get this part of the work done. "Can you come tomorrow afternoon?"

"I'll be here." He gazed at her with worry. "Fannie, if this work is too much for you…"

"*Nay!*" she said quickly. Despite her ambivalent feelings, she wanted to continue to work with him. The thought of not spending this time with David bothered her. "I'm fine." She blinked up at him. *"Okey?"*

His expression softened, and his blue eyes took on the gleam of happiness. *"Gut.* I'll see you tomorrow then."

Fannie watched him leave before she went inside the building to grab dinner for her father and Alta. Then she locked up and headed home.

Light rain splattered on the roof of the buggy Thursday afternoon moments after Fannie and David had delivered and mailed the last of the invitations. The wind picked up making it difficult to keep the buggy on the road as they headed back to the luncheonette. David turned up the speed on the windshield wipers and concentrated on the road. A jagged bolt of lightning pierced the dark sky in the distance, followed by a low rumble of thunder, startling Fannie. She hated storms and was eager to get to shelter. The rain began to fall in earnest, lowering visibility. Hugging herself with her arms, she peered through the windshield, hoping to recognize where they were.

"David," she gasped when the buggy shook with the force of the wind. If the horse spooked, they could end up hurt or dead in a ditch on the side of the road.

"I know. Hang on. We'll get there." He stared past the glass through narrowed eyes.

Finally, Fannie recognized where they were. "David, the luncheonette is on the left just ahead."

"I see it." He looked relieved although she could tell he hadn't lessened his concentration, for the storm was fierce and the rain was torrential.

Fannie met his gaze and tried not to show her fear. "We can use the storage building in the back of the restaurant with enough space for two or three buggies. I park my horse and buggy inside when there is a chance of rain. Pull your buggy to the right of it, and we can seek shelter inside in the luncheonette until the storm passes. I'll make us something to eat." The horse would be safe, and they would, too.

"Okey." After steering the horse into the parking lot of Fannie's Luncheonette, David drove around the back of the building to the storage structure.

Three separate open spaces looked similar to stables in a barn. Fannie's pony cart was parked in the one on the far left. David carefully eased the horse-drawn buggy into the one on the far right. The middle unit remained empty.

Once inside the shelter, Fannie got out quickly to secure the horse to a huge metal O-ring attached to the wall. When David's vehicle was secure, she went over to check on her mare. Jenny was skittish, but Fannie was able to calm her by laying a blanket over the horse's back.

"There are some towels on the shelf in the middle unit. We can use them to dry off your gelding." Fannie hurried to get them and handed him two towels. She kept two for herself. A clap of thunder made her gasp and turn away from the opening of the outbuilding.

David's horse neighed and shook. Fannie flinched each time there was a flash of lightning followed by a rumble of thunder as she wiped the water off the left side of the animal while David dried the right side. When they were done, she offered him the blanket.

"I think he'll be fine without it, but *danki*." He tossed his straw hat inside his buggy.

She nodded. "Let's get inside. I have more towels there for us if we need them." Which they no doubt would. There was an umbrella in the corner of the outbuilding near her pony cart. Fannie kept one there and one inside the restaurant. She picked up the umbrella and met David's gaze. With the whipping velocity of the wind, she wasn't sure if the umbrella would hold. "Ready?"

He inclined his head. They moved toward the open end of the outbuilding and hesitated as the rain slanted in the direction of the wind.

Fannie opened the umbrella. "I don't know if this is going to work."

David took it from her hands. "We should leave it here and make a run for it."

A bolt of lightning in the distance made her cry out.

"We'll be fine." David put his arm around her and held her close. "Are you ready?"

She nodded, and then the two of them ran into the storm toward the main building. The wind buffeted against their sides, slowing them down. It pulled on the bobby pins holding Fannie's head covering. A sharp gust tugged off her *kapp*, and she caught a quick glimpse of it as it sailed across the parking lot. *"Nay!"* she cried, unintentionally jerking away from David as she stopped and touched her bare head.

"Don't worry," David said in her ear as he surrounded her with his arm again. "We'll find it later." He pulled her closer and sheltered her with his body as they continued forward. Soaked from the downpour, they finally made it to the back door. There was a small overhang but nothing big enough to shelter them.

Lightning flashed across the sky, followed by a thunder boom that sounded close. David released her so that she could open the door. Frightened, Fannie struggled with the key until the lock finally clicked, and the back door swung open. She immediately stepped inside, pulled him into the building with her and slammed the door shut. Relieved that they'd made it, she turned on the lights in the hallway, kitchen and dining area.

"Have a seat," she said as David followed her into the front dining area. Fannie smiled at him, grateful they were in a safe place. "*Danki*, David."

His blue gaze brightened as it held hers. Awareness rose between them as Fannie stared at him, conscious of his dripping wet hair, face and clothes. She was just as soaked. Touching her hair, she knew that it was a mess. It seemed too intimate to stand before David without her *kapp*.

"Would you like something to drink?" Fannie tried to act casual when she felt anything but. The raging thunderstorm scared her, and she felt vulnerable. "David?"

He blinked and then smiled, releasing the sudden tension between them. "An iced tea if you have it."

Lightning lit up the room with a bang. The lights inside flickered but stayed on.

Nodding, Fannie tried not to panic. She could find relief in the kitchen, couldn't she? Cooking had always been calming for her, but then she'd never cooked during a storm. Still, she needed something to take her mind off the weather—and the man who filled her head with memories and confusion.

"Would you like a sandwich or a meal?" she asked. "I'd have both."

She watched him take a seat at a table in the back of the room, close to the kitchen.

"Whatever is easier." He frowned. "I'm concerned about my parents, who'll be worried about me."

"I'll call Mary and let her know where you are." Fannie understood. After what had happened to their son, his parents would fret every time David wasn't with them. "Mary gave me her number."

David gave her a wry smile. "Of course, she did."

"After what happened to you, I understand that they're afraid something will happen to you again." Fannie pulled out her phone from her apron waistband. "I'll let them know where you are and that you'll be home as soon as the storm passes."

His sudden grin took her by surprise and increased her heart rate. "*Danki*, Fannie."

Heading toward the kitchen, she dialed Mary, who picked up on the second ring, and explained the situation. David's sister sounded relieved and she promised to let her parents know that her brother was safe.

Fannie hung up and reentered the dining room. "There, that's done! Now your family won't worry." She glanced up from her phone to find David watching her intently.

The warmth in his smile extended to his cerulean blue eyes. "I appreciate it."

She nodded. "How about a roast beef sandwich on rye bread with mayonnaise and a side of potato chips?"

"Perfect." The hint of laughter in his expression made Fannie catch her breath. This David was a lot like the man she'd fallen in love with years ago. "You remembered."

"I did." She headed toward the kitchen again.

A bright flash through the window curtains illuminated the dining room, making Fannie gasp and freeze. A startling clap of thunder resounded, sounding closer than before. The rain fell in torrents, slashing across the wide glass panes across the front of the building.

"The storm's getting worse." Fannie turned and her gaze locked with David's. She hoped he couldn't see how afraid she was. "I'll make those sandwiches."

She was trying to remain calm. She hated storms, and not only because it'd been storming the day her mother died. When she was a small child, she'd got caught in one, the wind, rain, lightning and thunder terrifying her until her father had reached out through the rain and darkness to pick her up. He'd carried her into the house while she sobbed against his wet shirt. Dat hadn't realized that she was outside when the storm had hit, but once he had, he'd run out to find her, shouting her name to be heard above the storm. And then her fear had become so much worse on the day of her mother's death.

"Fannie. Fannie?" David's voice penetrated the frightening memory.

She blinked. *"Ja?"*

He studied her with concern. "Are you *oll recht*?"

She managed a smile. "I'm fine. I'll be right back." Pushing back the fear, she went into the kitchen, the one place she always found soothing, to prepare their food.

Chapter Ten

David was surprised by how quickly the storm arose and how fiercely. He'd been nervous for a second until Fannie had pointed out her luncheonette and the place behind it for his horse and buggy. Now they were safe inside the restaurant, and she was in the kitchen making a light supper. She came out moments later, carrying a tray with their sandwiches and drinks as he listened to the sound of the wind and rain against the building—and tried not to feel alarmed at the thoughts whirling in his head.

Fannie placed the food and drinks on the table and then left with the tray.

A bright flicker of lightning. An explosion of thunder. Fannie screamed when the lights went out as she entered the room.

"Fannie!" Forgetting every thought but those of her, David searched the darkness to find the frightened woman who'd become a good friend to him. The area brightened with a streak of white light and then he saw her a few feet away. He rose and caught her hand. "It's *oll recht*. We'll be fine." Leading her with their fingers entwined, he pulled the chair out next to his and tried to get her to sit.

She resisted. "I need a flashlight." Fannie looked terrified.

"I'll get it if you can tell me where it is." He pressed her gently onto the chair.

Fannie popped up. "*Nay!* Let's go together."

"Show me," he said.

To his surprise, she took hold of his hand and led them into the much darker hallway to the kitchen on the left. Fortunately, there was a curtainless window in the kitchen in the far back. David could feel Fannie tremble as she tightened her grip on his hand. "It should be in that cabinet." She gestured to a tall wooden cabinet. She released him and opened a cabinet door, which revealed a pantry and other kitchen supplies. He immediately spied the flashlight and two battery-operated lanterns on the top shelf.

"Let's take all three," he suggested.

Fannie lifted the flashlight near the edge of the shelf but couldn't reach the lanterns. She turned on the flashlight as David, at least a head taller than her, grabbed both lanterns. After setting them down on the closest surface, a kitchen worktable, he turned a knob until the lamp had been switched on to its brightest level. "No sense turning on the other one if we don't need it." Still, he carried them both out to the dining area with Fannie closely following, her fingers clutching the back of his shirt.

The sounds of the storm lessened, and they relaxed and began to eat. The roast beef sandwich was delicious, and he enjoyed every bite between tasty sips of iced tea. He sat back after he'd finished eating.

Fannie met his gaze and appeared self-conscious as she tucked her hair behind her ear. "Dessert?"

"Sounds *wunderbor*. You pick." David grinned and watched Fannie leave the room, clutching the flashlight. There was something about her that seemed so familiar. Was it because he'd been spending so much time with her, planning his parents' event?

The storm must have circled around, because it suddenly hit again with the force of a hurricane. At least, it sounded like he imagined one would sound. He rose and looked past the curtains outside. It was windy again, and the rain teemed, making visibility nearly impossible, but he could tell that as far as the wind was concerned, they weren't in danger. The flick-ers and flashes of bright lightning made him dizzy. As he stared through the window, lightning split a tree in two. David dropped the curtain and went back to his seat with the beginning of a light headache until he heard Fannie cry out with alarm. He grabbed the lantern and ran for her. He found her huddled on the floor in the kitchen below the dessert case.

"It's *oll recht*, Fannie. We're fine," he soothed as he gently pulled her to her feet. "Lightning hit a tree across the road."

Fannie looked shell-shocked. She couldn't stop shaking. Worried about her, David pulled her into his arms and whispered soft words of encouragement as he held her close. The storm abated somewhat. The winds continued, but the thunder faded to distant rumbles. Suddenly conscious that he had a woman within his arms, he slowly released her and stepped back.

She didn't meet his gaze, and it was just as well. He felt out of sorts, and he didn't want her—or him—to feel embarrassed or uncomfortable.

"I think the worst is over," he said quietly.

Fannie looked at him, her eyes filled with relief. "I hope so." She smiled. "I picked out chocolate cream pie..."

"Sounds *gut*." Suddenly, he was hit with a memory—brief, unrecognizable images flashed through his mind. He mumbled something about waiting in the dining room for it, and sat down at their table. He felt the sharp pain in his head again, but this time it was worse and constant, forcing him to lean over the table and hold his head.

"I think you'll love this pie—" Her voice cut off when she saw him. "David!" She set down the plates and hurried to his side. "You have another headache!" she whispered with alarm. "How can I help?"

He could only moan in answer.

"I'll be right back," she said softly. "I can help you."

David closed his eyes and quick flashes of images filled his mind. A navy four-door car. Three angry dark-haired men. The open trunk of a car. The look on the men's faces when they saw him. And then there was nothing but blackness.

As he sat with his head almost touching the table, David felt wet warmth settle on the back of his neck. One of Fannie's compresses. Then he heard her gentle voice. "It's a wet kitchen towel." She adjusted it to cup his neck with the ends dipping down his shoulders. "I also brought you some ibuprofen and a glass of water."

"Sick to my stomach," he muttered.

"I understand," she whispered. "I'll put it aside until you can take it." Her concern wrapped around him like a warm blanket, soothing him.

Lightning lit up the room followed by a thunderous crash. Not again. He was afraid this time he wouldn't be of much help to her. Fannie cried out then began to breathe harshly. David managed to lift his head to check on her. She had closed her eyes, and when she opened them again, Fannie met his gaze, as if she hadn't been frightened, as if her concern for him remained front and center.

"David..."

He pushed himself upright. "I'll be *okey*." David picked up the pills and swallowed them with a sip of water. Fannie's eyes filled with tears, and he was stunned by the depth of her worry for him. "I'll be fine, Fannie," he assured her.

"You're hurting. I don't like to see you—" she bit her lip "—*someone* hurt." She sniffed and turned away. "I'll be right back." Fannie left and returned a few moments later with a bowl of steaming water. After removing the towel from him, she reheated it in the water and quickly, carefully, squeezed out the excess. "Lean forward a little," she instructed. After he did, she placed the reheated cloth against the back of his head. She laid a dry towel over his shoulders before she held another wet one against his forehead. "There is still hot water left."

He gently grabbed her free hand. *"Danki,"* he murmured.

"You're *willkomm*." Her voice was a breath against his exposed head, ruffling his hair as she gently gave his hand a squeeze.

David inhaled sharply and then released it. He managed to control his intake and outtake of air while Fannie stood close to him, keeping the wet heat against the stress-tightened areas of his head and neck. She removed the towel from his forehead. And he nearly groaned out loud when he felt her fingers dig into the muscles along his shoulders and upper back. If the storm continued to rage around them, he didn't hear it. Fannie seemed unaffected by it as well.

Relaxing under her ministrations, David felt his headache ease. He sighed and sat back, catching the damp cloth on his neck before it fell onto the floor, unexpectedly brushing Fannie's arm in the process.

"Are you *oll recht*?" she asked huskily.

"*Ja*, much better. *Danki*, Fannie. Once again, you knew what to do to help me."

"We're friends, David. That's what friends do for each other." Her smile didn't reach her eyes. "Do you think you feel well enough for some pie?"

He could still hear the rain against the glass. They would have to stay here for some time yet. Now that his headache had lessened, his nausea had eased. "*Ja*. I'd love some."

The pie's texture melted in his mouth. The chocolate filling was rich and creamy with a decadent fudge flavor that teased and then satisfied his taste buds. The whipped topping added an extra boost to the deliciousness of the dessert. "Fannie, this is the best pie I've ever eaten." He grinned, feeling much better. "But don't tell my *mudder*."

Fannie laughed. "I won't. But I'm sure your *mam* makes *wunderbor* desserts."

The tenseness created by the storm and his headache eased. They chatted and chuckled as they finished their dessert and drank the fresh refills of iced tea that Fannie fetched for them. The lights in the restaurant flickered and then came on. They realized then that the thunder was much farther in the distance, and they couldn't see any lightning. The storm had left for good.

"I'll clean up while you head home." Fannie grabbed their plates as David stood and picked up their glasses. "You don't have to do that," she said.

"I'm not leaving yet. You fed me. The least I can do is to help you clean up." He followed her back to the kitchen.

"You don't owe me anything." She stacked the dishes in the sink. "The dishwasher is full of clean dishes."

"Let's wash these, then we can empty the dishwasher," he said, "so you'll be ready for tomorrow morning when you open Fannie's."

"David..." She seemed ready to argue.

"Please let me do this for you. You're working with me on the reunion, and you got rid of my headache." And he wasn't about to let her stay behind on her own. When he left, he would follow her to make sure she got home safely. Sometime during their ordeal, he'd felt something he'd never felt before. *Protective*. The feeling he wanted more than friendship with her, although he fought to control it.

If only he could get his memory back. He wanted more time with Fannie, including after the reunion when their business together was done. Unfortunately, he had no idea what his future would bring...and he wouldn't bring someone else into all that uncertainty.

Fannie locked up the restaurant. She turned and saw David waiting in his buggy, ready to leave. She frowned as she approached him. "What are you doing here? Why haven't you gone home yet?"

He regarded her with bright eyes that seemed to see into her soul. "We haven't set up a date to discuss the menu for the reunion."

"*Ach*, sorry! Why don't we get together next week? We can talk after Sunday service to set up a date. I'll see you then, if not before."

He nodded but didn't move.

"Why aren't you leaving?" she asked, confused by his behavior.

He smiled. "I'm waiting for you. I'll be following you home to make sure you get there safely."

"That's not necessary." She scowled when he appeared amused.

"I think it is. So I suggest you get into your pony cart and allow me to do this."

"David—"

"I'm not budging on this, Fannie," he said gently, but firmly. "We've had a trying day, and neither one of us feels like ourselves. I need to know that you got home *oll recht*."

She opened her mouth to argue.

"*Please?*"

And Fannie realized that she couldn't say no when he used that sweet tone of voice. She sighed. "Fine."

The grin he gave her affected her heart rate. *"Danki."*

It wasn't long before they were on the road toward her father's house. She couldn't help feeling a bit miffed that David didn't trust her to get home safely. But then she recalled the storm and how comforting he had been when she'd been frightened. They'd gotten a lot done as far as the reunion was concerned. All the invitations were out, and she hoped the partygoers would respond sometime within the next two weeks. They had used her cell phone number as a contact number for questions and RSVPs.

The closer she drove toward the house, the more guilty she felt for arguing with David. He had suffered more than she had during the storm—getting one of those horrible headaches. Fannie was grateful she'd been able to help once again.

She turned on her right blinker and pulled onto the lane that led to the house. Reining the horse to a stop, she glanced back toward the road and saw David wave at her before he continued past the property.

There was still much to do to prepare for the reunion. She and David needed to decide on a menu; she could provide David with a taste testing so he could make an informed decision on the food. But she wouldn't think about that now. She'd see him on Sunday for church service. And Saturday morning she was due to meet with Robert Steele about the upstairs bathroom.

As she parked near the barn, the door to the house opened, and her father stood there, waiting, looking worried. *Ach nay*, he was upset and she couldn't blame him, but she'd had no way of letting him know where she was. Jonas Miller refused to get a cell phone. Perhaps now she could convince him to get one.

"Dat, I'm sorry I couldn't let you know. David and I were delivering invitations when the storm blew in. We sheltered in Fannie's until the weather settled and I could drive home."

Her father pushed open the door to allow her in. "Did you eat supper?"

"*Ja*, I made sandwiches." She could feel the tension in her parent's frame. "Dat, there was no way to get a message to you..."

He sighed. "I know. But I couldn't help but worry about you."

Alta turned from the stove with a tea-kettle. "Fannie," she said as she checked her over. "You're *oll recht*."

"I'm fine." She saw dishes in the drain rack. "I'm glad you ate. I'm sorry I didn't bring you anything from the restaurant."

"No reason to be sorry. You don't have to cook for us, although we appreciate it when you do." Alta opened the refrigerator door. "Are you hungry?"

"*Nay*, I've eaten, but *danki* for asking." She faced her father, who eyed her intently, making her feel like a young, scolded child. "Dat, you should seriously think about getting a cell phone for emergencies. I could have called you."

Something softened in Jonas Miller's features. "I'll discuss it with Deacon Thomas."

Cell phones were not only good for business reasons but also vital in an emergency. If it hadn't been for the weather keeping her and David at the luncheonette, her father wouldn't have been concerned. But Fannie understood that her father was thinking how terrified she was of thunderstorms. "We had to stop."

He placed his hand on her shoulder. "I know."

"I'm sorry I made you worry." She held his gaze.

"I'm your *vadder*. It is my job to worry." Her *dat* then studied his wife, who was pulling mugs from a kitchen cabinet. "Alta is making tea. Want a cup?"

She smiled. *"Ja."* Fannie watched Alta bring a plate to the table. "Cupcakes?" Despite the sandwich and pie she'd eaten earlier, the sight of Alta's cupcakes made her hungry again.

"Ja." Alta turned from the table with a shy grin.

"I'd love a cupcake." She noted the pleasure in her stepmother's green eyes.

"Gut." She smiled at her husband. "Jonas? Take a seat, and we can enjoy our dessert with our *dochter* who is safely home."

As she ate cupcakes and drank tea, Fannie thought of her *dat*'s reaction to her late return home and hoped he took her suggestion to avoid his worry in the future. Dat knew that she'd been delivering the rest of the invitations with David today. She'd told him before she'd left for work early that morning.

Spending time with him had brought back memories of when they'd started seeing each other in secret. Fannie had always thought him handsome, but having his recent attention, seeing his smile directed at her and enjoying his masculine scent—soap, outdoors and a scent that was uniquely his—had captivated her. He was still the kindhearted man from their past, comforting her through her fear of storms.

Fannie had to fight her memories and focus on the present. She had a business to run, and she couldn't get lost in what she'd once had with David. His vulnerability shouldn't draw her to him. He was a grown man, not a boy, and he would find a way to move forward and recover from his amnesia. And it wouldn't matter when he did. She'd suffered too much to go back to where things were before she'd started Fannie's.

Yet, something inside of her whispered that she couldn't admit the whole truth about her feelings for David to anyone... including herself.

Chapter Eleven

Robert Steele met her at Fannie's on Saturday morning as scheduled. The man was pleasant while they discussed what she wanted in her future upstairs apartment space. He stayed about fifteen minutes and told her he'd call her cell phone with an estimate by the end of the day. She was excited for the start of the renovations.

"How expensive do you think it will be?" she'd asked.

"Not too bad. About a thousand dollars," Robert had said. "I'll figure it out and let you know. It might not be that high."

Pleased that Jed had recommended the man, Fannie thanked Robert before he left, and she headed home. She had cooking to finish for the shared meal after service tomorrow. Fannie smiled. She did so love her time in the kitchen preparing food.

Later that day, as she was outside enjoying the fresh air after cooking desserts for several hours, Robert Steele called her.

"Eight hundred even," the man said by way of greeting. "Call me back to let me know if you want to go ahead with it."

"Thank you," she said, giddy with the price that was more than affordable. Ten minutes later, Fannie couldn't wait any longer and called Robert back. "I'd like to hire you. When can you do the work?"

"I've got a busy work schedule during the week," he said, "but if you don't mind me working this weekend, I can start this evening. I believe I have all the supplies I need, so I should be able to finish the job tomorrow."

Tomorrow was Sunday, but Fannie knew that not every Englisher attended church or followed the no-work-on-Sunday rule. "I need to give you a key. What time do you want me to meet you?" The more she thought about the renovations, the more excited she became at the prospect of having her own place.

"Are you at the restaurant now?" he asked.

"No, but I can be there in a few minutes." And she wanted to grab a few things from the pantry.

"I can meet you there in fifteen minutes."

Fannie agreed before she hung up the phone with a smile on her face.

"What are you smiling about?" Alta asked as Fannie entered the house.

"It's a *gut* day. Why wouldn't I smile?" Fannie washed the last of the dishes in the sink. Then she dried and put them away. She turned to watch Alta carefully storing her cupcakes in a plastic container at the kitchen table. "I've got to run to the luncheonette for a bit. How do you feel about chicken potpie?"

"I love it, but you don't have to cook for us." Alta met her gaze with affection.

"It's already made. I hadn't planned on serving it on Monday, so it should be eaten. I meant to bring it home earlier." Fannie grabbed her purse, where she'd placed her keys. "You'd be doing me a favor."

Looking amused, Alta shook her head. "Fine. You're a sweet girl, Fannie Miller. I'm grateful to have you in my life."

"Dat and I are the ones who are grateful. I can't imagine our lives without you."

Tears immediately filled her stepmother's green eyes. *"Danki."*

"I… I'd like to call you *mam* if it's *okey.*" Fannie didn't know why it had taken her so long to tell her. The memory of her late mother was still with her, but the happiness brought into the house by Alta had made Fannie love her more than she'd ever imagined.

Sniffing, the older woman nodded. "I... I never thought I'd be this happy again."

Feeling emotional, Fannie's eyes also filled with tears. "You deserve to be happy. And my *vadder* deserves you."

"You have no idea how *wunderbor* it feels to have another *dochter*. A kind, sweet young woman whom I love."

She hesitated, reluctant to leave. Her *dat*'s house was a home filled with love and acceptance. Would Dat and Mam be upset with her once they knew she was planning on moving out? Would they believe she wasn't happy here? "I'll be back in a bit."

Her tears didn't stop as she left the house and climbed into her pony cart. By the time she reached her restaurant, she'd stopped crying, but there was a lump in her throat that made it difficult to swallow. Fannie enjoyed living with her parents. Just because she wouldn't be living in the same house didn't mean she couldn't see them whenever she wanted. She felt that it was best to give them privacy, and she liked the idea of becoming an independent woman and business owner. Besides, if she'd married, she'd have had to leave her father's home, wouldn't she? Thoughts of marriage brought on memories of David. They'd been young and in love with their entire future before them. Which turned out to be one day of pure happiness before her world imploded the next morning.

Fannie pulled into the lot behind her building. Robert Steele drove in a few minutes later after she'd unlocked the door and gone into the kitchen. Through the window, she saw him get out of his truck and approach. She let him inside. "Thanks for doing all of this so quickly."

"You're welcome." The man smiled. "Jed told me about you and this place. He said the food here is good."

"That's nice to hear." She grinned. "Do you like desserts?"

"Who doesn't?" He looked at his surroundings. "Why do you ask?"

"How big is your family?" She opened the dessert case and reached to the bottom shelf and removed a full apple crumb pie. "Will this be enough?"

His eyes widened. "More than. There are only four of us."

"I'll leave this here on my worktable for you," Fannie said as she carefully set the pie down. "Please take it home and enjoy it with your loved ones." She dug a key out of her purse. "Here."

He accepted the key. "Thanks. I thought I'd get to work now if it's all right with you."

"That's fine." She went to the refrigerator in the back of the kitchen and retrieved the large bowl of Amish chicken potpie. Fannie saw Robert with a tool belt around his waist as he pulled out a number of two-by-fours from the back of his truck.

Robert leaned them against the side of his vehicle. "Don't worry. I already did most of my cutting and if I need to trim anything, I'll do it out here."

Fannie nodded. "If you need another day to finish up, I close up the eatery at three thirty during the week. You can come back any day through Friday after then."

"I'll keep that in mind. Have a good night, Fannie, and thanks again for the pie." He picked up the studs and carried them inside.

She left moments later in her buggy with the potpie set safely on the floor of the passenger side with her purse. Feeling a renewed level of enthusiasm for her apartment, Fannie drove home.

The congregation had gathered for church service at the home of the Jonas Millers. Seated in the men's section with his father and brother, David closed his eyes and prayed for forgiveness, assistance and to regain his memory. He wanted a future and needed his past back.

Seated in the women and children's section with Alta on her right and his mother and sister to her left, Fannie looked lovely in her royal blue dress, white top garments and prayer *kapp*. Over these last weeks during their time together, he'd felt a strong connection with her…as if he already knew her inside and out. But that wasn't possible.

David had no idea if Fannie felt the same way. He took comfort in the realization they'd shared something special while they'd taken shelter from the storm. He'd offered her comfort from her fear of thunderstorms, and she'd done the same when he'd suffered one of his excruciating headaches. Closing his eyes, he recalled how wonderful and right it'd felt to hold her in his arms.

As if his attention drew her, Fannie glanced his way and smiled. His heart thumping at her expression, he had to remind himself that now wasn't the time to consider changing their relationship. Over the weekend he'd had flashes of memories.

David was afraid to hope. Some of the images he'd seen had been too disturbing to contemplate. Maybe one day soon he'd remember everything, and nothing he recalled would prove to be the least bit frightening to him. Only then would he be able to try for more than friendship with Fannie. With eyes closed, he offered up a prayer to the Lord that his fear wasn't based in reality. He needed a change in his situation soon.

Jonas Miller opened the service and continued after the other preacher had spoken briefly. David listened, sang and prayed, hoping for a miracle.

For him, the service seemed to fly by. After Preacher Jonas gave the service's closing remarks, members of the congregation began to file out of the room. David stood and followed his father and brother as they worked to move benches and set up tables in the great room for the midday meal. Because it was a beautiful day with temperatures in the low eighties, his father told him earlier that church members would have the option of eating indoors or outside.

The windows in the Miller house were open, allowing in the warm summer breeze. With the tables for dining and food in the house, David went outside to see if he could help with the furniture setup in the backyard. But the men were done with the work there. After debating what to do next, he looked for Fannie as he returned to the house. As expected, he found her in the kitchen pulling dishes and platters from the refrigerator.

"May I help?" he asked softly from behind her. She gasped, lifting her head, banging it against the shelf above where she'd been working. "I'm sorry! Are you hurt?"

She straightened, her face red. "I'm fine. Just embarrassed."

"Why?" David was curious. "I'm the one who scared you."

With a light laugh, Fannie blinked in his direction. "You're hardly frightening or a threat."

Warmth filled his chest. "I'm glad you realize that." He enjoyed hearing her laughter, and he felt happy simply by being near her. *Stop!* he scolded himself. *I can't allow myself to become too attached to Fannie!* David switched his attention to the dishes on the counter. "Where would you like these?"

"You don't have to carry those," she said. "There are enough women to do that."

As if to convince him, he heard the sound of female conversation as his mother, Mary, Lucy Fisher and Katie Bontrager entered the kitchen from the other room. Soon, the kitchen was a flurry of activity as the women moved into the great room with pitchers of iced tea and lemonade, and other dishes.

"See?" Fannie said as David stepped out of the women's way. "Plenty of help."

"Will we have time to talk later?" he asked.

"*Ja*, of course," Fannie said. "We have all afternoon. Let us get this meal ready, and we can get together after we all eat. *Okey?*"

"*Oll recht.*" Reluctant to leave her, David

decided it would be best to wait outside with the men.

David's family—along with Fannie, her parents and the Adam Kings—ate in the house. The rest of the congregation chose to eat outside, although everyone needed to fill their plates inside. David was conscious of Fannie seated at the other end of the table. His mother sat next to her and his sister next to his mother.

He finished his meal and stood, ready for dessert. After tossing his paper plate into the garbage can in the corner of the room, he went to the dessert table. There was a huge selection of sweets. David studied them and wondered which ones were made by Fannie.

"If you like lemon bars or frosted brownies, I'd go for one of those—or both if you'd rather," Fannie said as if his thoughts of her had drawn her to him.

He picked up a plate and flashed her a smile. "Yours?"

Her blue eyes twinkled. "Just two of many on the table."

With tongs, he carefully picked up one of each. "What else did you make?"

Fannie pointed to three other desserts— a cherry pie, a tray of whoopie pies and a decadent-looking coconut and vanilla layer cake. "How about I take enough of the others so we can share?"

David grinned. She was not only beautiful but charming. He quickly picked up another one of the three items on his plate. "Works for me." He glanced back at the table. "Where should we go to eat these?"

"The front porch? We have some chairs there with tables in between." She jerked her head toward the hallway. "Follow me."

Gladly. He followed her outside and watched her take a seat and place her plate on the wooden side table. He sat in the chair on the other side of it before he set his plate down where they both could reach it.

David picked up a lemon bar and nibbled on it. "Mmm. This tastes like a burst of citrus bliss in my mouth."

"That's sweet but odd." Fannie laughed. "But I like it."

There was a great deal of food between them. David continued to take tiny bites, hoping to prolong his time with her. "What do you think it tastes like then?"

She took a bite and tilted her head as if considering. Her expression triumphant, she looked at him. "A lemon bar."

David laughed out loud, completely taken with the woman and her teasing. "What shall we try after this?" He knew they needed to set up a time and date to discuss the reunion menu, but for now, he was happy to simply be. "What do you suggest?"

He watched Fannie study the two plates. "Brownie or a whoopie pie."

"I plan to try everything here between us," he said. "But how about the choco-late-frosted brownie?" He felt as if he'd won a prize when she beamed at him.

"Let's do it." She reached for one of the treats.

David picked up the other one and ate

some. "Wow. These are *wunderbor*. They melt in my mouth."

"I'm glad you like them," Fannie said after she swallowed her first bite. "Are they good enough to serve at the reunion?"

The hand holding the brownie froze on its way to his mouth. "Is this a dessert taste test?" he asked, dismayed with the idea that she'd brought their work on the reunion to the midday meal after service. A time when he preferred to simply enjoy treats together.

She shook her head. "Of course not. I plan to bring you into my luncheonette and bombard you with so many samples you won't be able to keep track."

"Seriously?" Was she teasing him?

"*Nay*. Just wondering about what you like."

I like you. David sighed. "I guess we should set up a time to discuss the menu."

"Tuesday?" she suggested. "I need a day, at least, to prepare food for you to try." She finished her brownie, and there was a full minute of silence as they both ate. Then she reached for a whoopie pie. "I don't know if I can eat all of these desserts."

"Then it's a *gut* thing we're sharing." David grinned. "Don't you think?" He sampled the whoopie pie. "Outstanding. That's three desserts with my vote yes." He watched her eat several bites of whoopie pie. "So, we'll meet on Tuesday. Same time as before? About four?"

"Sounds *gut*. If anything changes, I'll call Mary to let you know." Fannie stared at the table. "We forgot drinks."

David stood. "I'll get them. Iced tea?" She nodded. "I'll be right back. Don't go anywhere."

"I won't go anywhere." She offered a teasing smile. "I'm too lazy to move."

He was back within seconds with their iced teas. "Now that we have our next meeting set, why don't we enjoy the day?" *And each other.*

She nodded. "What should we talk about?"

"Anything you want to discuss, Fannie Miller," David said with warmth in his heart. "Anything at all." He closed his eyes briefly and drew in the sounds and scents around him. He could detect the delicious smell of her desserts. Mostly, he was aware of the woman by his side and the familiar scent of soap and vanilla shampoo. Vanilla… His stomach lurched as a glimmer of memory surfaced briefly and was gone. There was something about the scent of vanilla that stirred something in his thoughts. What he wasn't sure. It had come and gone too quickly for him to grasp on to it.

Chapter Twelve

Fannie spent her Monday doing what she loved—cooking for her customers. It was a help that Linda and Esther were working today, for she wanted to get started on making some of the food for her meeting with David the next day.

"Esther, did Linda tell you that we've been hired for a big catering job?" she asked. "I have to hire more full-time employees, but you'll always have a part-time job here if you're interested in keeping it."

Esther nodded. "*Danki*, but I was going to ask you if you would hire me full-time." There was a sadness in her expression that had Fannie curious, but she wouldn't ask for information that Esther might not be willing to give. "I've decided to quit the cleaning business."

Fannie smiled. "I'm happy to hire you full-time if that's what you want." It was seven thirty in the morning and she went to unlock the front entrance. She didn't want to be too nosy and ask why Esther had given up cleaning houses.

A flicker in Esther's green eyes. An averted glance. "I've decided that I'll clean for a friend, but that's all for now. I don't mind helping someone like you, but to clean for just anyone?" She sighed. "Let's say it's not how I thought it would be. And I always enjoyed working here, so…"

"I love having you here, so *danki*." Fannie shot Linda a glance. "The three of us can discuss a work schedule later. There is no reason for all of us to put in long hours if we are catering a small gathering. We may all have to pitch in for the larger events."

"We are both willing to work whenever you need us," Linda said after exchanging a look with her sister.

The two sisters headed out and took care of customers. Linda and Esther wrote down orders and served the meals that Fannie cooked. Whenever the front dining room became too busy for Linda and Esther alone, Fannie went to quickly assist before returning to the kitchen.

By the time the day came to an end, Fannie realized that she still needed one more employee. She decided that on her way home, she'd stop at Kings General Store to talk with Rachel about hiring her visiting cousin, who would be staying in New Berne for some time.

Linda with Esther cleaned up the tables and renewed the place settings for tomorrow. Soon, the sisters left, and Fannie stayed to cook food for David to try the next afternoon.

Two hours later, she was done for the day. First, she went upstairs to check on Robert's work on her apartment and was shocked that Robert had finished the job in a day and a half. He'd left his invoice and her key on the vanity sink with oak base in the bathroom. After looking over his bill, she was surprised but pleased to note a price lower than his last quote. She headed downstairs, grabbed her phone off her worktable and dialed Robert Steele. "Robert," she greeted. "Your bill is only for seven hundred and fifty."

"I know," he said, and she heard him chuckle. "I found a capped-off water connection just below the downstairs ceiling and the floor upstairs. Apparently, the last owners planned to do something with the second-story space but never did. That capped connection saved me time."

Fannie was amazed by the man's integrity. "Robert, you could have charged me for it anyway."

"That's not how I do business," he told her gruffly.

"Thank you. Where can I bring you a check?" Fannie examined the invoice and noted where his office was. She recited the address, and he confirmed its correctness.

"No hurry." She could tell he was smiling.

"I'd like to treat you to breakfast or lunch. Whichever you'd prefer. Just let me know. In the meantime, I'll get a check to you either tomorrow or on Wednesday. Will that be all right?"

Robert agreed, and Fannie told him how much she liked what he'd done and that she would see him soon.

Pleased with how her day went, Fannie checked the restaurant, making sure the stove was off, the front entrance was locked and the Closed sign was in place. Everything was as it should be. Then she grabbed her purse and left through the rear door and locked up.

Tomorrow she'd finish work on two possible menus and then call her suppliers to make sure she could get what she needed and that it'd remain affordable for Joanna and Samuel.

She had her apartment, her desserts and a number of dishes ready for David for tomorrow afternoon…and Esther King was her new full-time employee, someone who was already trained in what to do. All that was left was to talk with Rachel about her cousin's arrival, and if Rachel thought Hannah Lapp would want to work for her. Since it was later than she thought, Fannie decided she'd talk with Rachel later in the week. Fannie headed home, feeling good about the way things were going at that exact moment in her life.

The next afternoon after the restaurant was closed, Fannie came out from the kitchen to check the front dining room. It was close to four o'clock, and David would be here any minute. She noticed through the front window that it had started to rain. A steady drizzle coated the roads and sidewalks and added a sheen to the leaves of the large tree and the lawn across the street. She worried about David, and hoped he hadn't decided to walk here.

As the rain came down in a mist, Fannie wondered if she should take her buggy to look for him.

She went past the kitchen to the back entrance as she debated what to do. She hadn't parked in the outbuilding, because there had been no chance of bad weather. Opening the door, she studied the rain and the distance across the wet parking lot to her buggy. She hurried outside with an umbrella and moved her horse-drawn pony cart into the storage shed. As Fannie exited the building, a buggy pulled into the lot. She gestured for him to park inside the outbuilding and waited for him.

"Fannie!" He smiled as he approached.

She grinned and held up her umbrella, inviting him to join her. "You made it!"

David dipped his head as he stepped close to join her. He smelled of soap, man and the outdoors—scents she enjoyed. The wind suddenly blew mist beneath their rain covering. "You didn't think I'd walk here, did you?" he asked as they moved quickly toward the restaurant.

"I'd hoped you wouldn't." She opened the door and stepped back. He grabbed hold of its edge and gestured for her to precede him before he followed her inside.

"Are you ready for the tasting?" he asked as he shut the door behind him, closing them both in.

She nodded. "Let me get us something to dry off with." After grabbing some towels from a closet in the main kitchen area, she handed one to him.

"Danki," he said as he began to dry his arms.

Fannie frowned, feeling a chill. "I can make some hot tea to warm us."

"No need." He shook his head, his

brown hair scattering droplets of water, making her laugh. He grinned.

She dabbed the towel over her prayer *kapp* then rubbed it over her arms and down her legs beneath her dress hem. "I set up everything in the dining room. Come with me." She was happy when he trailed behind her. "I have prepared a number of dishes for you to try." Fannie led him toward a table where she'd used the fancy place settings she typically brought out for special occasions like a pre-Thanksgiving dinner.

She saw him shiver. "We're both wet and cold. I think we're going to need that tea." Fannie was pleased to have him here with her. There was something cozy and familiar about being inside a room with David on a rainy day when there was no threat of a storm. She felt a painful pang in the middle of her chest as she realized that she could have had many more times like this one if David had never left or never gotten hurt.

* * *

David followed her and widened his eyes when he saw how nicely she'd prepared for his tasting. "Did you think I wouldn't come because of the rain?"

"I didn't want you to walk in this mess, and I feared you'd already started this way and got caught in it." She examined him as if to ensure that he was all right.

He saw concern enter her expression. "Don't look at me that way, Fannie. It's like looking at my mother or father worrying about me." He shook his head. "Stop! I'm fine. I'm wet, not sick."

"Okey." She smiled as she pulled out a chair for him. "Have a seat and I'll be right back." And then she left the room.

David studied the table setting after he sat down. The plate looked shiny and new. He picked it up and realized it was breakable. After setting it down carefully, he leaned against the chair back and waited.

Fannie returned from the kitchen with a tray of drinks. "Here you go." She gave him a hot beverage and then placed her teacup before her chair across from him. "Water," she said as she gave him a tall glassful. "I suggest taking a small sip of water between food samplings."

He nodded, and she left again, returning seconds later with a meat platter.

"For the first course, I have hot roast beef," she said in a prim and proper voice that made his lips twitch with amusement. "Gravy will come on the side. You have your choice of sweet and sour green beans or baked corn with mashed potatoes. I have both vegetables for you to try. If you don't care for mashed potatoes, I can provide potato salad—Amish style or German." Fannie studied him with an expectant look.

He grinned. "Is there a reason you're acting so formal? We're friends, and my family has already hired you. Just bring out whatever you want me to try, and then we can discuss it. *Okey?*"

To his amazement, she blushed. "Sorry. I was trying to be professional."

"Save it for your other customers, Fannie," he replied with a gentle smile. "You don't need it with me." He saw her swallow hard.

"Oll recht." She turned to leave, and he caught her arm, stopping her.

"Fannie, it's just me. Relax. We've spent enough time together lately." He recalled the storm, and the look that came to her blue eyes told him that she remembered it, too.

"I'll be right back," she whispered, and he sighed. Had he made things worse rather than better?

Fannie returned with two vegetable bowls. David enjoyed watching her as she carried them to the table. The aroma wafting from the roast beef and vegetables made him briefly close his eyes and sniff appreciatively.

"That smells and looks *wunderbor*," he said.

Pleasure changed Fannie's pretty features into a face that he'd always thought amazing but now appeared breathtaking. He watched as she placed a sampling of meat, sweet and sour green beans, and baked corn on his plate. "I have mashed potatoes in the kitchen. I'll be right back with them in case you like to mix your corn with your potatoes."

Fannie brought out the mashed potatoes, and David added them to his plate. The food was more than delicious, and David complimented her cooking. "These are all a 'yes,' as far as I'm concerned, if we decide to go with hot food. Do you think hot food is best, or should we stick to cold?"

"I have chafing dishes, which will keep the meat and vegetables warm," she told him. "You can have hot and cold selections if you'd like."

For the next hour, David sampled two more kinds of hot meat—chicken and ham. She told him about other selections she could make. Then, Fannie brought out small sandwiches of different kinds. The tiny rolls were arranged artfully on a round platter. He liked the sandwiches of all types but told her that full-size rolls cut in half would be better, especially since it was likely the men would want to eat a whole one. He explained his reasoning, and she agreed.

After so much food, even in small quantities, David was too full to try anything else. "Can we stop for now? I didn't expect you to make so much food."

Fannie looked at him with alarm.

"I like all of it, of course, but I'm too full to eat another thing." He patted her arm as she stood next to him. "Everything was great. Let's get together again to discuss this, *ja*?"

She didn't pull away, and he enjoyed the warmth of her bare arm beneath her short-sleeved dress. *"Okey."*

David released her and stood. "Now we're going to clean up, and then you'll go home and relax with your family."

"You're acting bossy," she said. "I don't need your help cleaning up."

"Doesn't matter if you need help or not—I'm here, and you've been working and on your feet too long. I care about you, and I can't have you falling asleep as you drive home." He frowned as he wondered if she'd eaten. "You ate some of this food, didn't you?"

She shrugged. "I've been busy—"

"Fannie..."

"I'll bring some home and eat it with my family."

David smiled. *"Gut,"* he said, his voice soft. "Now let's get these dishes in the dishwasher, and then I'll follow you home." As predicted, she scowled at him. "I'll worry about you if I don't."

Her features softened. *"Oll recht."*

It didn't take the two of them long to stack the dishwasher with the plates and pans used. David watched as Fannie packed up some of the food—the roast beef, corn and mashed potatoes, so that she could take it home with her.

He grabbed two of the dishes while Fannie carried a platter and the pack of small rolls she'd used to make the sandwiches. David frowned when he saw her pony cart. "Let's put these in my buggy. We can unload them once we get to your *haus*."

When she opened her mouth as if to object, he just looked at her and then the two-wheeled pony cart and back at her again. Her expression cleared and she finally nodded.

David followed Fannie home and pulled onto the lane to her house. He watched her park her cart inside an open end of her father's barn, the one separate from where the man kept his dairy cows. After parking close to the back door, he waited for her to approach. Then he got out and handed her the meat platter and rolls. Following her up the steps, he carried the vegetable dishes and then handed them to her after she put the meat and bread inside.

"Have a *gut nacht*, Fannie," he said quietly. "You provided a delicious meal today. *Danki*. Call my sister when you want to get together again. Unless you want to schedule it for tomorrow afternoon?"

She gazed at him a long time before answering. "Tomorrow afternoon at four will be fine." Fannie turned to enter the house, and David headed toward his buggy. "David?" she called.

He halted beside his vehicle and faced her. *"Ja?"*

"I'm glad you liked my cooking."

David grinned. "I have yet to eat anything you've made that I don't like." Then he spun, climbed into his buggy and left with a smile on his lips. He knew that somehow, someway, he would overcome his amnesia. He had to. It was the only way he could entertain the idea of attempting to win Fannie's affection. *No past. No Fannie.*

Chapter Thirteen

Considering she and David delivered the reunion invitations last week, Fannie was surprised at the number of people who had already called her with a response. Everyone she'd spoken with so far had told her that they would be coming to the event. They had mailed only one invitation to a family in Indiana, and she imagined it would be another week at least before she heard from them.

She had met David the following afternoon as planned to discuss the menu. David told her that the variety of hot and cold food he'd tasted was perfect for the party. In his mind, there was no reason for him to taste more. As far as desserts, he trusted her to choose whatever treats she thought best. The only change to the food he'd eaten was the size of the sandwiches. He thought it best to use kaiser rolls, not the tiny slider buns or anything smaller. Some of those sandwiches could be cut in half for the guests who wanted a smaller portion.

The next few weeks flew by, and in no time it was the day before the event. Fannie hunkered down in her restaurant, preparing food. She made several large pans of baked corn and three bowls of sweet and sour green beans. The potatoes had been boiled and mashed with milk and lots of butter. She'd reheat them in the microwave right before heading to the Troyers with all the food.

Her father had gone to the Troyers' that morning with the church bench wagon. Her *dat* was a kind man who had offered to set up tables and seating in the backyard. Fortunately, the weather forecast for the day was sunny with mild temperatures and a light breeze. There would be no rain tomorrow.

Taking it upon herself to help keep the Troyers' guests entertained, Fannie had sought advice from an English friend, Bert Hadley, a kind neighbor who had lent her two sets of cornhole boards with beanbags, which he put into the back of her buggy. She'd seen them in a store in town once but she had never played. According to Bert, young and old alike would enjoy a fun-filled cornhole competition.

"Let's see," Esther said as she came out from behind the refrigerator. "We have the roast beef and vegetables ready to go. Since you decided at the last minute to make macaroni and potato salads, you can keep them cold in the inflatable ice holder you bought, *ja*?"

Fannie nodded. "I still have a number of sandwiches to make." She grinned. "Two beef roasts should be enough, don't you think? We won't use them in sandwiches. They'll be easy enough to keep hot in the aluminum foil chafing dishes."

"What time do you plan to be here in the morning?" Esther pulled five dozen eggs from the refrigerator and set them on the worktable.

"Too early for you." Fannie shot her another grin. When Esther arched her brow in question, Fannie laughed. "Five o'clock."

"Five," Esther echoed. "What time do we need to set up the food?"

"By eleven." Fannie filled a large pot with water and turned up the flame. She then prepared the eggs for hard-boiling by pricking one end of each one with an egg prick. "Hmm. Maybe I should come in at four."

"I can come in then, too, if you need me. I'm sure Linda can, too." Esther picked up the prepared eggs and eased them carefully into the warm water. She added a dozen and a half of them before she replaced the pot cover. "Where is my *schweschter*?"

"She's buying two big coolers and several bags of ice for me to carry the cold food in tomorrow." Fannie eyed the list of things she still needed to do. A delivery of kaiser rolls and rye bread was expected this afternoon. She had two types of cheeses for the sandwiches and cooked ham ready to be sliced. Maybe she should invest in a slicer. It would come in handy as their catering business expanded—and it could be used in the restaurant as well.

Fannie heard the back door open. "Linda?"

"*Ja*, it's me," Linda called.

"And me," a male voice added. *David*.

Linda entered the kitchen with two bags of ice, and David followed her in with two more bags.

"*Hallo*, David." Fannie grabbed one of the bags that Linda had brought in and placed it in the large commercial freezer, where she'd cleared space enough for four bags earlier that morning. She turned back to get the rest. *"Danki."* She smiled as David handed her one bag at a time and watched her put them away.

She and David moved back to the front of the kitchen.

Linda checked the eggs on the stove and found that the water had reached boiling point. Leaving the lid in place, she turned off the heat.

David smiled. "I want to help, see if you need anything done."

He followed her into the work area. "We're in *gut* shape. The salads are done. Oh, I didn't tell you about them. I made macaroni and potato salads—no extra charge. I thought they'd go well with the sandwiches. We're in the process of making egg salad. I have the meat and cheese ready for sandwiches, which we'll make in the morning." She faced him. "The hot meal will be ready for whenever your *mam* wants to serve it." Using the back of her hand, she rubbed away an itch on her forehead. "Did you see my *vadder*?"

"*Ja*, he's there now. My *dat* wouldn't let me help with the benches." He looked frustrated. "I may not be able to remember my past, but I'm healthy and well enough to carry a bench. I helped move them after service last Sunday."

"So you thought you could help out here." Fannie understood how upset he must feel. His family might not want him working in the yard or house, but she was happy to use his help. They'd worked well together over the past several weeks. Although there were times when David seemed to withdraw from her, lately they'd grown closer, even more so since the day of the thunderstorm when they'd been there for each other. She and David had formed a friendship and work relationship that would assure tomorrow's event was a success.

David sighed. "Are you going to tell me to leave, too?"

She chuckled. "And turn away help? *Nay.*"

He studied her as if he'd never seen her before, then he grinned. "Where would you like me to start?"

"You can begin by bringing in the new coolers." Fannie nodded toward the door. "And then I'd consider it a big help to organize the refrigerator and freezer spaces. We have a lot of food to make and store."

"On it." David moved to leave. He paused at the kitchen archway. "Fannie."

She frowned. *"Ja?"*

"Danki." A spark of gratitude seemed to brighten the blue of his eyes.

Her expression softened. "I should be thanking you, David. You're the one assisting me."

David woke up late on the day of the reunion, feeling anxious. It had been a long night of worrying about the event. He understood that his parents were only trying to help him. But inviting so many strangers made things harder for him, not better. He'd spent an enjoyable Friday afternoon and early evening at Fannie's Luncheonette, helping wherever he could. David was grateful Fannie had found things for him to do. He'd worked hard and felt good about it. The work kept his mind occupied until late last night, when he couldn't fall asleep, and now this morning when he suddenly remembered why they'd been working so hard.

His parents and siblings were already up when David went downstairs for breakfast. Given the hour, he was surprised that they hadn't already eaten. "Something smells *wunderbor*!" David smiled at his mother when she turned from the stove with a frying pan.

Mam grinned. "It's scrambled eggs mixed with potatoes and onions."

"My new favorite," he said, and was surprised when his mother's expression turned wistful.

"It was your favorite before, too," Mam

said with a sad smile. David knew each day that went by without him conquering his memory block hurt his mother and his father...his entire family. It made him feel terrible for everything they'd suffered through because of him.

"Take a seat, Bruder." Simeon sat at the table with a cup of coffee.

David grabbed his usual chair next to him. "What are you doing up so early?"

"It's not early. I'm always up at this time," Simeon said with a smirk. "Here, I made you a cup of coffee. Don't worry, it's still hot."

He smiled his thanks and felt his brother's gaze on him as he fixed the brew the way he liked it. He took a sip. "Perfect. *Danki.*"

Simeon snorted. "The pleasure is all yours." But then he flashed a genuine smile to show that he'd been teasing. "Are you ready for our company?"

David hesitated before answering. "Truth?"

Seated at the head of the table, his father eyed him intently. "*Ja.* Always."

"I'm feeling…off-kilter." David accepted the plate of food his mother gave him. "Since I was released from the hospital, I haven't felt comfortable around a lot of people."

Simeon's brow creased. "But these are your family and friends."

"And I don't remember or know any of them." He took a sip from his coffee.

"We hope that you'll recognize at least some of them." Dat studied him with concern. "If it gets too overwhelming for you, *soohn*, find a place somewhere to enjoy a few quiet moments alone."

David could only nod, and soon everyone dug into breakfast. He enjoyed the cut potatoes and onion cooked right in with the eggs. His family discussed simple things like the chores that needed to be done today before the reunion.

"Where is everyone going to stay?"

David asked later when he was alone with his mother.

"Jed and Rachel King offered to put up a family of five and the Adam Kings said they could take in five or six people." His mother washed a dish and placed it in the drain rack. "But I think most people won't stay overnight, which is why we chose to hold the party at noon."

David picked up a dish, dried it and put it away. "I appreciate what you're doing for me, Mam. Please don't be upset if this reunion doesn't do what you want it to."

Joanna arched her eyebrows as she paused in washing a dish to meet his gaze. "What is that?"

"Spark my memories. I know that's why you decided to do this." David grabbed another wet dish and dried it. "It's been over two years, and I still can't remember my past." And the flashes he did remember had startled him…he wouldn't worry his parents with it.

His mother emptied the sink basin. "It

will happen when it is supposed to, *soohn.* Your memory will return with time."

He released a sharp breath. *I hope so.* "I thought I'd head over to the restaurant to see if Fannie needs any help. There is a lot of food to transport. I thought I'd take the market wagon so between her vehicle and ours, we can move everything in one trip."

"That sounds like a fine idea." She smiled. "Fannie is a kind young woman."

His heart started to beat rapidly. "I thought so from the first time I met her."

"She's lovely." Mam continued to study him with a softness in her expression.

"Mam, don't...*okey*?" He shook his head. "Fannie and I are friends, and that's all we can ever be." Didn't his mother realize that in his present state he wasn't good for any woman, even one as sweet and caring as Fannie Miller? Although he was certainly interested...

The smile left his mother's expression. "I just worry about you."

"I know. You've made that frequently clear." He was grateful for her concern.

"I love you, *soohn*."

"I love you, too, Mam." He hung up the dish towel. "I'll be at the luncheonette, helping Fannie." His mother didn't say anything, and he knew he hadn't eased her mind.

David hugged his mother and then left. Fannie would need all the assistance he could give her since it was her first catering job.

When he pulled into the parking lot, Fannie and her two employees were loading the back of her market wagon. He pulled his family's wagon behind Fannie's before he jumped out.

"Gut mariga!" He found himself grinning when he met Fannie's gaze. Just a short time ago he'd felt like a wreck, but something about this blonde woman with the blue eyes calmed him. He realized that after today they wouldn't be working together anymore. He was going to

miss spending time with her. This morning Fannie looked hassled, and he wanted to alleviate her stress.

"I've come to help move the food." David jerked his head toward his vehicle.

She blinked then sighed. "*Danki.* I shouldn't accept, but honestly, I can use the help."

The other two women had gone back inside. Without conscious thought, David gently took hold of Fannie's shoulders. "Everything will be fine. Your food is amazing. We've planned this together, so let's continue to work together until it's over and we've cleaned up."

Looking into her gorgeous eyes, he felt a jolt of something familiar. He gave her a little squeeze and then stepped back, feeling shaken. "Are the coolers inside and ready to go?"

Fannie nodded. "*Ja.* One is filled with ice. The other one has food."

"Lead the way," he said with a small smile.

David followed her into the kitchen and

immediately saw that she'd been busy. There were trays of artfully arranged sandwiches. In the center of each one, she'd added a container of pickle slices. He moved to take a closer look. "These look *wunderbor*, Fannie."

She beamed at him. *"Danki*, David."

He helped her carry everything needed, including a folding table. Once they filled up her wagon, they moved the items that remained into the back of his. Fannie drove to his house with Linda and Esther while he traveled alone.

Once they arrived, David climbed out and helped her unload. "My *mam*'s kitchen is ready for you. Her worktable is clear, and she made room in the refrigerator if you need it."

Fannie looked at him with surprise. "That's...*wunderbor. Danki*, David."

Fortunately, although it was early August, the weather was beautiful without the humid heat that sometimes took over the summer.

"Would you like me to set up the food

table?" he asked as he led her into the backyard to see how the tables and benches had been arranged for their guests.

He watched Fannie as she studied the layout. "It looks like Dat set up tables over there for the food," she said. "Is it *oll recht* if I set up the folding table in the *haus*?"

"*Ja*, of course. Come and I'll help you with whatever you need." They went back to their market wagons, where Esther and Linda were waiting patiently by Fannie's vehicle.

"Let's move everything inside, except for the plates, napkins and utensils," Fannie instructed.

David followed Fannie's lead. Soon, the food would be set out and their guests would arrive to join them.

Fannie studied the artful array of sandwiches and smiled as the Troyers' family and friends filled their plates with hot and cold food. She'd filled a five-gallon container with iced tea brewed early this morning. There were two more in the house in case they needed it. Joanna had provided a jug of lemonade with a spare inside.

She saw David exit the house, followed by Mary and Simeon. He seemed to hesitate when he caught sight of the crowd in his backyard. Then his gaze locked with hers, and he headed in her direction. Watching him make his way to her, a smile firmly in place, reminded her of a time when he made her feel special, as if she was his whole world. She felt a pain in the center of her chest for what could have been and never would be. A part of her inside admitted that she still might love him a tiny bit.

"David," she greeted, managing a smile. "Looks like all of your company is here."

He nodded, his expression sober. "I don't know any of these people."

She could only imagine how out of place he felt.

A young man approached where David stood. "David! It's *gut* to see you again. What has it been, five or six years?" He caught sight of Fannie, and he straightened. "Who is this?"

"*Hallo.* I'm Fannie, a friend of David's family. And you?" She hoped that he would answer so David would have an idea who this man was.

"James," he supplied with a wide smile. "James Hostetler. You may have met my *bruder* Lloyd." He faced David. "A friend, huh?"

She saw irritation flare in David's expression. "*Ja,* David and I are *gut* friends." Fannie held the man's gaze so he would get the message.

"Lucky man," James said. Someone called his name and James looked over his shoulder. "Sorry. Got to go. It was nice seeing you again, David. Fannie, it was a pleasure to meet you."

She nodded and watched him through narrowed eyes as he walked away. When her eyes met David's, she found a strange look on his face. "What?" she asked.

"*Danki.* I didn't know the man, and I

still don't." He gave her a crooked grin. "Maybe that's for the best."

Fannie laughed. "You can say that again."

"David." His mother approached from behind him.

"*Ja*, Mam?" He turned with a respectful look on his features. "Is there something you need?"

Joanna shook her head. "Do you recognize anyone? I saw you talking with James. He is a friend from our former church district. I never did…" She sighed "Never mind. You're not feeling overwhelmed, are you, *soohn*? If you feel that way, it's *okey* to escape for a while."

David nodded. "I'm fine."

His mother faced Fannie. "Everything looks *wunderbor*. You've done a great job with the food. I've had nothing but compliments from those who have eaten. You'll get my recommendation."

Fannie blushed. "That's kind of you to say so."

"She's not being kind, Fannie," David

said. "She's telling the truth. I've heard the comments myself."

A young woman came up the food line. She was pretty, with chestnut hair and bright green eyes. Fannie wondered who she was to David.

"David," his *mam* said. "This is Margaret Graber. She is also a member of our former church district."

David nodded as he studied her. "Nice to see you. It's been a long time. Forgive me for not remembering."

Fannie had to give him credit. He was respectful to Margaret without being over-friendly. She saw Margaret smile at him, the young Amish woman's beauty more than apparent. Focusing on the food table to ensure it was well stocked kept Fannie from thinking about David chatting with Margaret.

She was stunned by the stab of pain she felt at the thought of David with another woman. *He's not mine.*

And he would never be hers again. Which was what she wanted...wasn't it?

Chapter Fourteen

David meandered around the yard, meeting people he was supposed to know but
didn't. He smiled and attempted to look
happy that everyone was there. The only
thing he wanted was to go off somewhere
by himself. *To simply be.*

He saw Fannie by the food table, chatting with people as they filled their plates.
It was one o'clock in the afternoon, but it
seemed like much later. David fought the
strongest urge to visit with Fannie, but
he kept it in check. There was something
about her that soothed him. If he didn't
know better, he'd say that he had fallen for

her. But it didn't make sense. One didn't develop feelings for someone that quickly.

Someone yelled from a car as it passed by the property. *"Clip-clop! Clip-clop!"*

David stiffened. Flashes of images flooded his mind. *A yell. A scream. A struggle.* The flicker of visions came faster, overwhelming him. He closed his eyes and fought the urge to cover his ears as the harsh sounds reverberated in his head. He struggled to breathe but couldn't draw in enough air.

I have to get out of here.

He hurried away from the gathering toward the pasture and beyond, but could still hear the crowd in his backyard. Desperately needing quiet, David picked up his pace and headed toward the woods in the rear of his father's property. Finally, surrounded by a dense coppice of trees, he found his heart rate slowed and his ability to draw oxygen improved. He continued until he was inside a thicket where he found a fallen tree trunk. David sat down on the log, inhaled and exhaled deeply, and closed his eyes. Fragments of memories invaded his thoughts. *A navy four-door sedan. An open trunk. Three dark-haired Englishers as they beat then lifted a body into the back of the car.* And then the moment the trio of men saw him inside his buggy in the parking lot behind the store where he'd been waiting patiently for Mary. He'd realized then he was in trouble.

Harsh shouts. The men dragging him from his vehicle and throwing him onto the ground...a dark-haired man pulling him upright and then a fist slamming painfully into David's head. The stark burst of agony in his face and the dull excruciating smack of his head against pavement. Those final moments of suffering that felt as if they damaged every part of his body until his face and limbs swelled as he was wildly beaten. And then his world went black.

David had awakened in the hospital,

every muscle and bone screaming with hurt; yet, he learned the worst of it moments later. He couldn't remember his name or what had happened to him. He hadn't recognized the older couple gazing at him with terrible worry in their eyes or the girl and young boy who stared at him with fear…and concern…the family he didn't know.

The headache started as a sharp throbbing behind his eyes. David leaned forward to cup his head as the pain intensified to a heavy pounding. Inside his chest, he felt his heart race as sparks of light filled his mind with frightening pictures. His mind opened, and his past returned with a starkness that shocked him. He saw his sister and brother and his life as a child. He experienced his mother and father's affection as they raised him to the man he'd become.

Then he experienced a cooling breeze. *Comfort. The first time he'd met Fannie. Their friendship growing into something*

*more. Confessing his love for her. His re-
lief that she felt the same way. Asking if he
could court her, and her happiness when
she agreed.*

He sat upright with a gasp. How could
he have forgotten how upset he'd been
when his father told him the family was
going to New Wilmington because his
grandfather was ill and might die. *Fannie, I never wanted to leave you.* And that
early morning when they'd departed, there
hadn't been time for him to send word to
her. He had planned to call her as soon as
he could, to explain why his family had
gone without notice and that he would see
her when he got home. But then his life
had changed in an instant.

Every little detail about his attackers
came back to him in full force. About the
three men who'd left him unconscious in
a store parking lot. Each man's features
were now firmly imprinted in his mind,
front and center, distinctive in his mem-

ory. He could easily identify them. But could he take the chance?

Did they know he'd survived?

What if they were looking for him right now?

It had been two years since the attack, but there had been no news of a murder, or anyone being arrested for one, in New Wilmington afterward. He knew because his parents had told him that there were no clues to the identity of the thugs who'd assaulted him. The men must have gotten off scot-free. Which meant that if they ever found out David was alive, and where he was, he would be in serious danger.

His thoughts warmed as he remembered Fannie. The girl she was two years ago and the young woman she was today. Her beautiful blue eyes. Her quick smile. Her sweet kindness. David recalled every little thing about her, and he wanted nothing more than to have her back in his life again as his sweetheart...and then his wife.

He frowned. Fannie hadn't said a word to him about their love for each other in all the time that they'd worked together.

He leaned forward and cradled his head as he realized how much he must have hurt her when he'd left without a word. *How heartbroken she must have been!* He understood now why he'd developed feelings for her so quickly, because they'd had always been there, hidden. A love and affection for her that he was afraid to act on because he'd been a man without his past. They had developed a friendship during these last weeks. And they'd shared moments that he'd thought significant. Like those that occurred between them during the thunderstorm. A closeness he now realized he would never have with another woman. Because Fannie was the one. His beloved, chosen by God for his future. But what if she couldn't ever forgive him for leaving her without telling her?

Sorrow hit David hard. He felt the sting of tears as he realized that their time wasn't here yet. There was still danger from the men, his attackers, who might be waiting to hurt him. He couldn't put Fannie in harm's way. They were friends, and while he wanted more, he had to distance himself from her. At least for a little while. It was only right for him to protect the woman he loved.

She must have been heartbroken when he hadn't reached out to her after he'd left New Berne. Too heartbroken to give him a second chance once the danger went away?

He lifted his head, straightened and stared out at the forest green foliage, made darker for lack of sunlight that barely filtered in past the trees. Now that the door to his past had been opened, more memories returned with a vengeance...of him and Mary playing horse as children, him as the handler with a rope loosely around his sister's waist. Of the time he'd taught Simeon how to play baseball when his little brother was five years old. The way his little brother had looked up to him as if David was the sun, the moon and the stars.

David remembered heavy snowfalls when he and his father had shoveled the driveway to the road—and the time their buggy wheels had gotten stuck in the mud along the side of the road after heavy rain. He and his father had pushed the vehicle while his mother had worked the leathers.

Suddenly, the past came back too quickly, the memories racing one right after another, making it difficult to think. He groaned at the sudden painful pulsing at his temples, the wild racing of his heart. David dropped his head back into his hands and prayed to God for help, for safety for his family and Fannie. He breathed deeply in an attempt to get himself under control.

How he wished things were different! All he'd wanted was to regain his past, and now that he had, he'd discovered the knowledge only complicated his life more, not made it better.

* * *

From her position behind the food table, Fannie searched the yard. She hadn't seen David lately, and she was concerned.

"Linda, would you and Esther set out the desserts for me? I have something I need to do."

"Of course," Linda said. "Don't feel as if you need to rush back. We've got this."

"Danki." She made a quick check to ensure there was enough ice in the inflatable tray, which had been used for the salads with mayonnaise and soon would hold the cream pies she'd brought. Fannie smiled. "You've been a big help today."

Linda grinned. "It's been fun. This is the easy part. We all did the heavy work before we came."

"That we did." Fannie saw Joanna and Samuel. David wasn't with them. Alarm hit her hard. *Where is he?* "I'll be back as soon as I can."

Fannie looked inside the house first. She called his name, but he didn't answer. Her concern for him grew as she ran outside, back to the table. Where could he have gone?

"Is something wrong?" Linda asked, eyeing her with concern as if she could see right through her.

Fannie placed a hand briefly on the young woman's shoulder. "I'm looking for David."

Esther came from the area where their market wagon was parked. "Maybe he went for a walk."

Fannie nodded. "Maybe." She started to leave, then stopped and faced her friends. "I need you to know that I appreciate you—both of you. I couldn't have done this today without you."

"You never have to worry about us leaving." Esther set down the plates. "We're in this for the long haul." She grinned and turned to her sister. "Let's make room for the desserts."

As her employees got to work, Fannie continued her search for David. She wandered through the yard, her gaze sharp on her surroundings.

Joanna approached Fannie as she walked through the backyard. "You've done a *wunderbor* job with the food, Fannie."

Fannie smiled. "I'm glad you're pleased. Esther and Linda are getting ready to bring out desserts. I promise that when we leave, your kitchen will be clean and you won't see a trace of our current mess."

David's mother chuckled. "I doubt it's a mess. At least, not compared to the ones I can make." The woman eyed her with curiosity. "Is there something you need?"

"*Nay.* I thought I'd find David. He has been a big help with the event."

"I haven't seen him." Joanna frowned.

"Not to worry. I'll find him," Fannie assured her. "I believe you told him to seek time alone if he needed it."

Beaming at her, Joanna nodded. "*Ja,* you're *recht.* I did. Go find him, Fannie. I'm sure he'll be happy to share his time with you."

Warmth and a sense of belonging settled inside her at Joanna's kindness. "If you need anything, Joanna, please ask Linda or Esther. I won't be long."

"Take all the time you need." David's *mam* headed toward the food tables.

Moving toward the barn, Fannie breathed deeply. For some reason, she experienced the urgent need to find David quickly, and she didn't know why. *It's hard to forget what he once meant to me. What he still means to me.*

Since his time away from New Berne, he'd had a lot to contend with.

After she checked inside the barn and around the perimeter with no sign of him, she began to panic. Forcing herself to remain calm, Fannie ventured toward the woods at the back of the property. The trees were thick, and she hesitated before daring to go in.

"David?" she called softly, afraid that she'd stir up some wildlife when all she wanted to do was find the man she'd loved.

Fannie roamed through the thicket in her search. She'd go a little farther before she turned back. Her footsteps crunched on downed sticks and leaves as she continued through the underbrush, watchful for thorn bushes.

And then she saw him. The relief that hit her made her dizzy. David sat on a log with his head in his hands, his body rocking back and forth as if he was distressed or in pain. She approached him carefully; she didn't want to startle him. "David?" she whispered.

He jerked upward, his eyes wild, blinking rapidly until his expression cleared. But then he shook his head. "*Nay.* Go away," he gasped. "Leave me alone."

Stung, Fannie was unable to move. "David?"

He bent his head. "Now. Please go. I want to be alone."

Pain lashed inside her heart as she turned

to leave. She took several steps and then spun to study him. He looked miserable, bent over, his head in his hands again. *He needs a friend. I can't leave him.*

She approached him and sat on the log beside him without a word. He might not want her there, but she would remain a quiet presence, a friend. Fannie didn't look at him. She closed her eyes and listened. A scurrying sound had her opening her eyes in time to see a squirrel climbing a tree before disappearing into the leafy canopy overhead. She heard the breeze rustling the treetops. But it was the sound of harsh breathing that drew her attention. *David.*

Without looking at him, she touched his hand and then withdrew. She was prepared to sit for hours if needed. He shifted on the log. His breath evened out. Fannie could feel him relax and was glad she'd decided to stay. Because he was David Troyer, the man she still loved, even if nothing ever came of their relationship.

She didn't know how long she sat there, but it didn't matter. Joanna had told her to take her time, and Esther and Linda had the dessert table covered. Fannie became aware of the silence and more so of the man next to her.

David shifted again, drew a sharp breath and then released it. "I remember the attack...and why I was targeted."

Chapter Fifteen

David stared ahead as he began to talk. Fannie wondered if she should turn to face him then thought better of it.

"I was waiting in the buggy for Mary while she shopped for groceries," David said. "She was only getting a few things, so it didn't seem important for me to go inside with her..." He released a harsh breath. "She thought the same."

Fannie grew tense with concern while she waited for him to continue.

"I heard a sound—a commotion. I didn't know where it came from until I saw three Englishers beating a man, who struggled and cried out before he suddenly went silent. His attackers lifted his limp, bloody body from the paved parking lot and threw it in the back of a car. A navy four-door." She heard his increased breathing. "They were laughing as one man closed the trunk. I heard him say that thanks to them, Joe was no longer a problem." His breath grew ragged, and Fannie felt a sinking feeling in the pit of her stomach.

"One of them circled the car to get into the passenger side," he continued. "That's when he saw me. He said something to the other two, and the next thing I knew I was pulled from the buggy. I fell and hit my head and hurt my back, and one man—Dennis, I heard them call him, the only one I know by name—tugged me to my feet. Then all three beat me. I remember feeling terrible pain in my face, head and stomach as they hit me with their fists. They continued to punch me and then threw me to the ground only to grab me to stand again so they could continue to hit me." Fannie's chest felt tight as she listened to David recount the story. "The last thing I remember before I blacked out was their laughter and Dennis saying 'clip-clop, clip-clop' in a mean tone they all thought was funny..."

Clip-clop was a derogatory term some Englishers used to degrade the Amish. Fannie felt his shudder and it echoed her own. Knowing what he'd gone through... She blinked back tears. It was a miracle that he'd survived. She wished she could do something to ease his pain, hated that he still suffered because of what happened to him. "David..."

He went on. "I blacked out. When I finally came to, I was in the hospital." David's voice was even, without inflection. "My family—I didn't know them. I couldn't recall a single thing about my life before the moment I opened my eyes." She looked at him in time to see him close his eyes with a pained expression. "I almost died because I saw something they didn't want me to see."

She reached out to take hold of his hand and was upset when he shook off her touch. Fannie drew strength from the fact that David was upset and wasn't rejecting her. While he'd remembered his attack, he didn't seem to remember what they'd shared.

Fannie longed to comfort him, to pull him into her arms. "Do you know what they look like?" she asked softly.

"*Ja.* In detail." He met her gaze, his blue eyes filled with fear.

"You need to tell the police, David. I'm sure they have sought answers about the day of your attack. I know you may not want to, but think about these men hurting someone else." She saw she held his attention. "I can go with you if you'd like."

His lips firmed before he glanced away. "I can take care of it myself."

"*Okey.*" Blinking rapidly to hide her distress, Fannie swallowed against a painful lump. She stood. "I should get back to work." She started to walk away.

"Fannie." His voice reached her across the space separating them.

She halted and faced him. *"Ja?"*

David blew out a breath. *"Danki,"* he said. "For being a friend."

Nodding, Fannie continued toward the gathering, where she rejoined her workers at the dessert table. "Everything *oll recht*?" she asked with a smile that felt forced. David was her friend. She wished she knew how to help him. It would have been better if he hadn't remembered. She knew he'd wanted his past back, but the cost to him seemed too great now that the memory of the attack had returned.

Linda studied her and then nodded. "All is well. Everyone loves the sweet treats."

Fannie nodded. "We've had a *gut* first catering event."

"It's been a great day," Linda said, and her sister agreed.

It might have been a wonderful day for

business but not for David. She wanted him to be happy and at peace. She would be there for him and offer comfort...and pray that God would help ease his pain.

She'd left him sitting alone in the woods, but how could she not? Especially since he'd told her he didn't want her help. Fannie had no idea that he remembered every single little thing about her and their relationship. It didn't matter, though, because until his attackers were behind bars, she couldn't have a place in his life. Not as a friend nor the woman he loved. And she was both.

Tomorrow was Sunday. He didn't feel up to church or visiting, not after being immersed in a huge gathering of people at the reunion all afternoon. *I'll have to see how I feel in the morning.*

When David entered the yard, his father saw him and approached. "*Soohn*, are you *oll recht*?" He appeared worried.

He nodded. "I'm fine, Dat."

His brow cleared as he nodded. *"Gut."* With a sweeping gaze, his father studied their guests. "Do you recognize anyone?"

"Ja. There's Mam and Mary and Simeon. *Ach,* and there's Grossdaddi and Grossmammi." He grinned to show that he was teasing.

"Seriously, David," Dat said.

David shook his head. *"Nay.* I'm sorry but I don't," he said sincerely.

Samuel sighed. *"Ach,* well. At least, we tried."

"I'm sorry that you went to all this trouble." He felt terrible that his parents had gone to all this expense in the hope of his regaining his memory. As a memory trigger, the event itself had been a failure. It was the Englisher calling out *clip-clop* that had done it. He didn't want to tell his family what he'd remembered yet. They would worry about him more if he did.

"Dat, how long ago did I meet these people?"

His father gave it some thought. "When

you were much younger. Some of them we had at the house when you were older, perhaps a young teenager." He sighed. "We thought you seeing a cousin or aunt and uncle might bring back memories of your childhood."

"I'm sorry. I know you're disappointed. A few people from our old church district look familiar but that's all."

His *dat* studied him with amusement. "*Ja*, to be honest, I don't remember many of them either." He lowered his voice. "Don't tell your *mudder*, though, *okey*?"

David chuckled. "I won't." He and his father exchanged smiles until a relative gained his parent's attention. At least, David thought it might be a relative, but he couldn't be sure. He had a feeling that most of these family members he'd met when he was much younger than four, which was why he didn't know them.

He saw Fannie at the dessert table. Everything inside of him urged him to go to her, but he held his ground. Monday morning, he'd tell the police what he remembered and hopefully what the authorities needed to find and arrest the thugs. It had been two years. Would there be a chance to find the men who had beaten him until he was unconscious after all this time?

David felt bad for forcing a distance between him and Fannie. He didn't want to and he risked losing her. She had offered to go with him to the police, and he regretted turning her down. She wouldn't come to harm by going with him, would she? *Nay*. He reminded himself that he wasn't in New Wilmington. He lived in New Berne with his family. Despite his first concerns, he knew she'd be safe to visit the police station with him. Fannie thought they were friends, and he'd hurt her by pushing her away. He could take her up on her kind offer, something he desperately needed, before he had to let her go...until the brutes were securely behind bars.

Fannie stood alone at one end of the table. David strode with determination toward her, ready to apologize.

When he reached her, she met his gaze and flinched. He softened his expression. "Fannie, may I talk with you? It will only take a moment."

She glanced at her coworkers, who nodded. "Go ahead," Esther said.

He turned, hoping she would follow him as he walked away. After seeking a place where they could be alone and finding it behind the barn, David halted and faced her. "I'm sorry," he said hoarsely. "I didn't mean to be rude."

"David—"

"I was, Fannie. I was awful to you. After I remembered what I saw and the attack afterward, I was upset and scared."

Fannie eyed him with compassion. "I understand."

David knew she didn't know the full reason why he'd tried to push her away. To protect her. Because he loved her. But he couldn't tell her…not until it was safe for him to attempt to win her back. "You shouldn't." Closing his eyes, he inhaled sharply and then exhaled slowly. "I should have thanked you for being there for me. Instead, I pushed you away." He fought the urge to take her hand. "If you're still willing, I'd appreciate it if you would go with me to the police station on Monday."

She nodded. "Of course, I'll go with you." He leaned against the barn. "I'll have Esther and Linda open the restaurant. Everything is ready for the day. We can leave first thing. Will that be *oll recht*?"

"You don't have to change your day for me." He frowned. "We can wait until after you close the luncheonette."

"*Nay.* I think it best if we go first thing." Fannie faced him as she settled against the structure, too. "It's fine. You can come back for breakfast when we're done."

David nodded. Getting the visit over with sounded good. The memory of the attack hung over him like a heavy weight on his shoulders. Focusing on how lovely Fannie looked in a light blue dress that matched her eyes, he agreed that he should tell the police as soon as possible so he could move on. *"Danki,"* he whispered. He offered a silent prayer of thanks. His beloved was here because he needed her. Fannie was an amazing woman who was beautiful two years ago but even more so now. And she was still the same—kind, caring and giving. She had once given him her heart, and he prayed he'd get another chance to recapture and treasure it always.

"You're *willkomm*, David. I know that memory is hard and upsetting to you, but at least you remembered something, *ja*?" She blinked, and he immediately got caught up in how long and dark her eyelashes were as they brushed her smooth cheeks.

He fought the urge to touch her silky skin where the lashes touched. *"Ja*. It's *gut* to know something about my past when for so long I remembered nothing."

"I can imagine." Fannie straightened. "What time on Monday?"

"Eight?"

"*Okey.* Pick me up at Fannie's." She smiled when he frowned.

"Eight it is then." David straightened, eager to get back to the gathering. He enjoyed spending time in Fannie's company too much.

Fannie fell into step beside him until they returned to the reunion, and she left him to join her employees at the dessert table. David glanced over and saw all the sweets. He had a hankering for something chocolate. He grabbed a plate and then got into line behind five others. As he studied the offerings, he felt her presence beside him before she spoke.

"Chocolate?" Fannie smiled as she met his gaze.

David could only nod. The lemon squares and zucchini bars were picked over, leaving only a couple left on the plates. Fannie took his plate. "Trust me?" she asked.

He didn't answer, but he had given her his approval when he didn't grab back the plate. Fannie went down the line and put four items on the dish before handing it to him. One of them, he saw, was the chocolate-frosted brownie she'd given him during the tasting.

"Enjoy," she said, and then she left to help someone else, letting him know that she wasn't treating him any differently than one of the other guests.

When the event was over, Fannie and her workers cleaned up quickly and efficiently before they left. The yard was empty. The benches and tables had been taken down. David told himself he was glad it was over, but he wasn't. Because after Monday, when Fannie accompanied him to the police, he would have no reason to spend any time with her. The woman he'd wanted for his own.

The next morning he woke up with the

worst headache he'd ever suffered. It was bad enough for him to take his pain medicine. After assuring his parents that he would be fine while they went about their Sunday, David lay down and fell asleep. When he woke, his family was home from visiting, and he could hear them downstairs. He joined them in the kitchen, and his mother cried out when she saw him.

"David!" His *mam* had tears in her eyes. "You look pale. Are you *oll recht*?"

He grabbed on to her hands and held them gently. "I'm fine. Headache is gone."

His mother appeared relieved. "Are you hungry?"

He hadn't eaten all day. "*Ja*. Extremely. I've slept the day away, I'm afraid."

"Sit," she instructed with a wide smile, "and I'll feed you."

His brother, sister and father were eating sandwiches at the kitchen table.

"Nice of you to join us, Bruder," Mary said with a smirk. But he could see the concern his sister tried hard to hide.

"I'm sorry the reunion didn't help with your memory," Simeon said. "I'd hoped..."

Dat nodded. "We all did."

"I did remember something," he said, drawing everyone's attention. "My family. My childhood. I was alone taking some quiet time when everything we did as a family came back to me."

His mother cried out with joy. "David!"

David gave her a crooked smile. "I still didn't know anyone at the reunion."

Mam blinked then laughed. "That's *oll recht*. It's nice that you know us now."

And it was. He teased his brother and sister with recollections of when they'd played tricks on him. "Now that I'm aware, be careful. You never know how I'll get even."

Mary's face expressed horror. Simeon stared at him as if he was serious. And David laughed heartily. It felt good to understand exactly how he fit into his family. He sent up a silent prayer of thanks to God for helping him find his past again.

That night he slept well for the first time since the attack. Tomorrow he and Fannie would give information the police would need to start an investigation.

On Monday morning, Fannie was waiting for him outside as David pulled into the lot behind her luncheonette. He reined in his horse and then jumped out the driver's side with a grin. "Are you ready?"

She nodded but didn't wear her usual smile, as if she was worried about him. He helped her into the buggy and then hurried to get in on the other side. David tried to tease her, and for the most part, he succeeded until he saw the police barracks ahead and they both immediately grew silent. He felt the tension along his jaw and gripped the leathers until his fingers were white. A navy sedan parked in the lot next to the station made him jerk back on the reins. The horse slowed and then stopped at the edge of the lot.

"David?" Fannie's soft voice calmed him. "What's wrong?"

"That looks like the car the body was dumped in." His heart thumped hard as he tried to control the tension in his body, the slight ache that started in his head.

"But it probably isn't. We're in New Berne. Surely a similar car here is a co-incidence." She reached out to brush her fingers over his, which still clutched the reins. "Let's go inside. If it is the same car, we'll know soon enough."

David met her gaze and saw support, caring...and something that looked like love. He nodded. "*Okey*. I'll park and then we'll go in."

Because there were two large Amish communities in the area of New Berne, it was easy for him to find a hitching post for his horse.

He climbed out and then went to assist Fannie.

"Are you ready?" she asked, her voice and her expression soft.

Exhaling a heavy breath, David met her gaze and bobbed his head. He was grateful when she took his hand as they entered the building. "*Danki*, Fannie," he murmured as they approached the front desk.

The officer at reception looked at them. "May I help you?"

David gazed at him and said, "I need to report a crime."

Chapter Sixteen

The police officer looked skeptical as David told the story of what had happened to him in New Wilmington over two years ago. Fannie could feel how anxious David was and couldn't help placing a hand lightly against his back to comfort him.

"Why don't you contact the police department in New Wilmington?" Fannie suggested when there was a short lull in the conversation. "David suffered a severe head injury from the attack and just recently recalled the details of that day."

The officer glanced at her briefly before softening his expression as he studied David. "Come in the back. I'll see what I can do."

She heard David exhale heavily before she withdrew her hand as they followed the man—Officer Michaels—to a room in the rear of the building where there were three chairs and a table. The interrogation room? She'd heard of such things from her brother Danny, who had an English firefighter friend who knew all the New Berne police. Maybe she should have enlisted Danny to help David…

David sat down and Fannie took the seat next to him. He was too quiet. Was he upset that she'd spoken up? She only wanted to help and support him.

She felt the urge to apologize for interfering. "David—"

Officer Michaels entered the room, interrupting her. "I spoke with Sergeant Rhoades, who investigated the incident of an attack on an Amish man two years ago. You. He seemed pleased with the return of your memory. He told me he'd visited you in the hospital three times. You were unconscious for the first two. When he got back with you the third time, you were awake, but you were dazed and suffering from amnesia." He eyed David with compassion. "I'm sorry. I've never dealt with a cold case like this before."

"Cold case?" David frowned.

"Yes. It's when we investigate a crime but then have to abandon the case because there are no leads and nothing more we can do." Officer Michaels looked from David to her. "Is there anything else you haven't mentioned? You said the car you saw was navy blue, like the one in our parking lot but older. And that there were three men."

David nodded. "I remember hearing the name of only one man. Dennis."

The police officer's eyes brightened. "That could help." He smiled. "Rhoades is sending me the information he was able to obtain at the time. A sketch artist will be in to get descriptions of the men who attacked you. I'll also bring you a book of male mug shots. It would be helpful if you could go through the book, page by page, to see if you recognize anyone."

"Okey." David appeared ill.

"Headache?" Fannie whispered.

He shook his head and didn't look at her. She tried not to feel hurt until she realized that David was under an extreme amount of pressure. It wasn't every day that a person relived the worst day of his life years after it happened. He probably wasn't upset with her but with his current situation.

They remained at the police station for three hours. Fannie sat near David while he gave a detailed description to the sketch artist of each man he'd seen that fateful day in New Wilmington. As each drawing took on a likeness, Fannie could feel the tightening of David's shoulders and wished she had the right to take hold of his hand to soothe him. She watched as he studied each page of the mug book and saw his lack of reaction as he studied face after face in the book with no recognition. And then he gasped and pointed out a familiar face and the name below it. *Dennis Porter.* Seeing the name in print triggered David's memory of hearing it that awful day. "That's him!"

"Excellent," Officer Michaels said when David told the policeman when he returned to check on them. "The man has a rap sheet of larceny and petty crimes. The New Wilmington department will find him and bring him in for questioning. In the meantime, I'll see what I can find out about any known associates. If we can prove his guilt, then he'll be arrested and charged with assault and battery. And if you are right about what you thought you saw—a man beaten to death before his body was tossed by his attackers into the trunk of a navy blue sedan, it's possible he'll be facing a murder charge."

Fannie watched as David thanked the

man. She added her thanks and then followed David out of the police station. She was tired and could imagine how exhausted David must feel. It was close to lunchtime. It was too late for breakfast, but they could enjoy the midday meal.

He didn't seem inclined to talk, so she didn't speak to him. Until they got closer to Fannie's.

"David, did you want to come in? I'll make us each lunch." She waited with bated breath. Was she now linked to this horrible memory for him? All because she wanted to support him while he told his story?

"Okey," he said, glancing at her briefly.

She smiled, relieved. *"Gut.* I'll make us something tasty."

For the first time since he'd entered the police station, David relaxed enough to chuckle. "I'm looking forward to it."

But as they passed Fannie's Luncheonette to turn into the parking lot, she caught sight of a Closed sign on the front door.

Where were Linda and Esther? Why was the restaurant closed?

David hadn't seen the sign. As he pulled to the back and parked, Fannie saw Linda and Esther's buggy. The sisters were still here. Her heart beat wildly as a sudden sensation of dread dropped a weight into her stomach. She climbed quickly out of David's vehicle and ran to jerk open the back door. She stopped and gasped at what she found inside—the floor flooded with water. Because of the new plumbing upstairs? she wondered, stunned.

David came in behind her. His gaze fell on her before it widened as he took in the mess on the floor.

"Fannie!" Linda cried. "We had to close because the restaurant is flooded. I tried calling your cell phone and realized when you didn't answer that you must have forgotten it or turned it off."

Fannie saw the mops and buckets the girls had taken out. "How far?"

"In the dining room, kitchen...everywhere." Esther tried unsuccessfully to mop up water and squeeze it into a bucket.

David walked through the flood and checked the restrooms and a closet, which he opened. "Fannie, it's from your water heater. It looks like it burst, which caused the leak."

She nodded. So it wasn't because of the work done upstairs. Tears filled her eyes as she studied the mess and wondered how long her restaurant would be closed for cleanup and installation of a new water heater, something she hadn't planned for.

"I have an idea," David said. "I'll run down the street and rent a wet vacuum. It will make cleaning up easier. And I'll see about renting fans. The sooner we get this water up and the floor dried, the less likely that you'll have to deal with mold and mildew."

Fannie sniffed as she met David's gaze. The warm compassion she saw in his blue eyes calmed her. "*Danki*. I have a credit card you can use." It would be all right.

One step at a time. David was there to help. She retrieved her card and made a quick call to the rental business to tell them about her giving David permission to use her credit card.

After he left, she faced her employees—the sisters who had been a blessing to her and continued to be there for her every day. "I'm sorry."

"For what?" Linda asked. "It's not your fault this happened. Do you know how old the water heater is?"

"*Nay*. I thought it was fairly new when I bought the place." Which was over a year ago. She stepped through the water to look into the appliance closet that held not only the water heater but the heating and AC system. Fortunately, the water didn't reach the unit because there were blocks underneath it. Fannie became alarmed at a thought. "The electricity!"

"We turned it off at the circuit breaker," Esther said. "I'm glad you showed us what to do in the event we have a partial power blackout."

Fannie released a harsh breath. "*Danki*. That was quick thinking." She shuddered to think that two of her closest friends could have been electrocuted. Linda and Esther looked like they were about to drop. "David will be back to help me. Why don't you go home? You've worried and done enough for the day."

"We don't mind staying," Linda said, and her sister agreed.

"I know you don't," Fannie replied with a sad smile, "but both of you have been *wunderbor* and deserve a rest. I'll see you on Sunday. I don't know when we'll be able to open Fannie's again." She studied her surroundings. "I'm hoping we won't have to be closed long."

After much convincing on Fannie's part, Linda and Esther left. David showed up within minutes. He came through the back door and propped it open. He had rented not only the wet vac and three big fans but a generator. He also brought gas and extension cords. He handed back her credit card with the receipt.

"I thought it best to turn off the electricity and use the generator instead," he said. David eyed her with sadness. "I'm sorry this happened, Fannie."

"Me, too." Fannie watched him set up the wet vacuum first. Some of the water escaped through the open door. Using her cell phone, she dialed Robert Steele and explained the situation with the leaking water heater. Robert promised to stop by within the hour.

The sound of the wet vacuum sucking in water was like the hymnal music that was sung in church. Fannie prayed that everything would be fine. And that David's attackers would be caught soon and David would stay safe. Watching him work to get rid of the water in her place of business brought on an intense rush of love for David. Despite all the pain and heartbreak she'd suffered after he had left, Fannie couldn't stop her heart from beating for him. Because his amnesia wasn't his fault. She knew he didn't remember her, and she understood that he might never be in her life like he once was. But to have him for a friend was better than not having him in her life at all.

David took care of the water in the back first, paying extra attention to the kitchen since the place where she prepared food needed to remain clean and germ-free. When he was done, he moved to the front dining room. He had to stop multiple times to empty the wet vac. Fannie quickly placed a fan in the kitchen and propped open the restroom areas and appliance closet. Using an extension cord, she plugged the fan into the generator outside and felt relieved to hear the noisy whir of its motor. She had attached a second fan and carried it toward the dining room as David was coming out.

He grinned at her as he dragged the wet

vacuum behind him. "Dining room is all done."

Fannie stopped and battled tears as she tried to smile. "*Danki*, David. You're a *gut* friend." She saw his expression change but only briefly. Had she imagined it or did he seem upset that she'd called him a friend?

Whatever disappointment she'd thought she'd glimpsed in his expression was gone. Fannie set up the fan in the front room and turned it on. The breeze from the electrical appliance was strong, and she had a feeling that it wouldn't take long for the dining area to dry out.

When she headed toward the back entrance, David was plugging in the third fan. He looked up at her approach. "Let's put this one in the hall. We can start it in the restrooms then turn it to dry the rest of the area."

"Sounds like a *gut* plan." Fannie felt sick at heart. Everything she'd worked so hard for seemed in severe danger...until David had jumped in to help her. It was strange how only that morning she'd been a friend and support to David, and now he was doing the same thing for her. "I need to call my *vadder*."

Fannie rubbed a hand across the back of her neck as she checked out the floors, which were quickly drying. The only thing left to do was replace the water heater and then have an electrician come in to inspect all the outlets and the power supply.

Her father arrived when they were finished doing what they could for now. "Fannie..."

He studied his surroundings and shook his head. "I'm sorry, *dochter*. We'll get this fixed. Your *bruders* and I will help you paint."

"I'd like to help, too." David was taking in everything as well.

"*Danki.*" Fannie approached where both men stood. "I can make us lunch. Is anyone hungry?"

David smiled. "I am."

She eyed her father. "Dat?"

"I've eaten, but I appreciate the offer." He narrowed his gaze as he studied the walls.

"Let me know if you change your mind," she said. "There are leftover sandwiches—roast beef, chicken salad and turkey. They're all *gut*. I kept them cold during the reunion and afterward. I also have a container of potato salad that was part of the special for today." She glanced at David and grinned. "I have potato chips."

His eyes held laughter as he chuckled.

"I'm going to look around," her *dat* said, "to figure out how much paint we'll need."

"Dat, you don't have to do that now. We can't paint until after the electricity is checked and we have a new water heater."

Her father faced her with a concerned expression. "That's fine. I want to see how much damage was done."

Fannie nodded. "Feel free." She turned back to David. "It's damp and chilly in here. Shall we eat outside?" There was a picnic table in the back between the outbuilding and luncheonette where she and her employees enjoyed their breaks and ate lunch whenever the weather was warm enough and they could find the time.

"*Ja.* I think it best." David followed her into the kitchen and helped her by taking roast beef sandwiches and potato salad out of the refrigerator and shutting it quickly to retain the cold inside.

They ate and drank iced tea in the warmth of the summer sun. Fannie experienced a lightness she hadn't known since learning of what had happened to David during the attack. She stood and collected their paper plates—which David had insisted on since without power she couldn't run the dishwasher. Robert Steele pulled into the lot and parked close to the door.

"The plumber," Fannie told David as Robert climbed out of his truck.

"Let's check your water heater," the man said, and went inside like he knew where everything was—which he did since he'd already done the work upstairs for her.

David raised his eyebrows.

"Jed recommended him," Fannie told David, and he nodded as if he understood and followed her into the building. He waited in the dining area to survey the damage at her request, while Fannie took care of business with the plumber.

Robert eyed the contents of the closet and jotted a few things on paper. "You need a new water heater," he said as if the expense wouldn't be a hardship for her.

Her father came out from the dining area to see Robert inspecting the offending unit. "Meet Robert Steele, Dat," Fannie said. "Robert, this is my father."

Robert smiled. "Nice to meet you." He shook her father's hand. "I'm sorry that it's under these circumstances."

Fannie leaned toward the appliance to take a look. "I figured we'd need a new one."

"I'll write you an estimate." Robert eyed

the pad with his notes. "You'll have it first thing in the morning. And I can check out your electric outlets and heating system, too, if you'd like. I'll add the cost to the estimate."

"Thank you." She was suddenly tired. It was as if she'd gotten up in the middle of the night and had lived a lifetime since then.

"Are you pleased with the bath upstairs?" Robert grinned.

She froze and shot a quick look at her *dat*. "It's just what I wanted. Thanks again."

"Bathroom?" her father said in an undertone no one but she could hear, while Robert picked up his tape measure. "Why do you need an upstairs bathroom?"

"I—ah—I'll explain and show you. Do you mind if we talk later?"

But Jonas Miller's expression had taken on a hard look.

"I'll explain," she said. "I promise." Fannie was relieved when her father nodded. But it was clear that he wasn't happy.

David had overheard the plumber as the man discussed the work that needed to be done. He felt terrible for Fannie. He knew that the flood would force her to close the luncheonette for a time and that she was devastated by the damage. Fortunately, they'd been able to clean up the water, and if the fans worked properly, it wouldn't be long before the floors and baseboards dried.

Fannie saw the plumber out and then returned moments later. She met his gaze with a sigh. "Dessert?"

"Something chocolate?" he teased.

"Of course." She watched him for a minute until he agreed.

She brought out a chocolate cake with creamy fudge frosting. Fannie cut into it, and he saw that between the layers was a white creamy filling along with dark chocolate. She sliced two big pieces. "More iced tea?" she asked when she turned with dessert plates in hand.

"I still have some, but *danki*." David followed her outside to the picnic table. He sat on the bench across from hers and smiled when she set the rich dessert before him. He ate a forkful and made a sound of pleasure. "This is delicious, Fannie." He watched her take a bite of cake. "Where did you learn to cook? You're *gut* at it. Your *mudder*?"

"*Nay*. Mam didn't enjoy cooking. She did well enough, but I... I enjoyed everything about it. I learned a lot in the last couple of years." She faltered as if she'd said something she shouldn't have.

"I appreciate you sharing your talents with me." David hadn't known until he'd entered her luncheonette his first full day back in New Berne about Fannie's talent for creating wonderful dishes. Of course, he hadn't remembered her then. It was only a couple days ago that the memory of her and their relationship returned along with the stark, horrific details of the beating he'd suffered at the hands of three evil Englishers.

He was awed by her, how she'd created a successful business and was so compassionate toward others. Being in her company warmed and comforted him with a yearning to recapture what they once had.

"It's a pleasure to share food with you, David." Her smile seemed sad. "Everything you did to help today... I would have been more upset if I hadn't found comfort in knowing you were working beside me to clean up the flood."

"Fannie, you stood by me quietly while I relived the worst day of my life. You were a friend when I needed one. So we must be even, *ja*?" He ate more cake and then grinned. "This dessert is worth wading through a foot of water."

She looked sick at the thought. "Praise the Lord that the water wasn't that deep." Fannie glanced toward the building. "My

Dat is still inside, and I need to talk with him."

David held her gaze steadily and nodded. "I'll stay here and wait for you." He watched her go and sent up another prayer that his attackers would be caught and arrested soon. He wanted to be a vital part of Fannie's life again...if she'd let him.

Fannie left David outside and entered the building. Her father stood with arms crossed, waiting for her. "*Dochter*, what did the plumber mean when he mentioned an upstairs bath?"

She swallowed hard. "Do you have a moment? I'd like to show you." Fannie felt nervous as she grabbed her key for the new door Robert had installed at the base of the stairs.

"Of course." While he waited patiently for her to continue, there was a look in his eyes that told her that he was expecting the worst.

"Please be open-minded with what I'm

about to show you. *Okey?*" She headed toward the door that led to the staircase and unlocked it. She could feel her father's stare bore into her back as she ascended the stairs and entered the large space she'd chosen to make into an apartment.

Fannie stepped inside and waited for him to join her. She watched as he took in the open second-story space, and then his expression hardened when he saw the walls that Robert had constructed in the corner. "What's this?" He appeared confused.

"It's an apartment." She swallowed hard when she saw his eyes widen. "There is no bed or anything in it yet, but it does have a bathroom with sink and shower."

Her father stopped his study of the room to pin her with a glance. "Why?"

"Dat, I love you and Alta. You're newlyweds and you don't need me around..."

"You want to move here?" He clearly wasn't pleased. "By yourself?"

"It's the best solution. I spend a lot of time here anyway..."

"Nay!" he exclaimed angrily. "I can't allow it."

"Dat—"

"Nay! No *dochter* of mine is going to live alone ever, especially when there is plenty of room in my own *haus*." He looked disappointed in her, but still, he softened his voice. "Fannie, your home is with us."

"You don't deserve for me to be underfoot for the rest of my life. I most likely will never marry. I promise I'll still bring food for you and Alta—"

"I said *nay*, Fannie." His tone brooked no argument. "You will obey and not cross me in this."

Fannie felt the sting of tears. "I just want to do what's best."

His features softened. "What's best is for you to live at home. With us."

"Maybe I could fix it up more. Rent the space?" And get back some of the money she'd spent adding the bathroom.

Her father shook his head. "You can't rent this space to someone else. An employee might be able to use it, but the King girls reside at home with no plans to move from their parents."

"Dat…" She couldn't believe this. Why couldn't he see that this was the best solution for all of them?

"How much did you spend?" Dat watched her carefully.

She reluctantly named the figure, and he nodded. "I'll give you the money."

"*Nay*, Dat! This was my choice." Tears spilled from her eyes to drip onto her cheeks. "You've done too much for me already."

"You are my *dochter*, Fannie. My little girl."

"But I'm not little anymore, Vadder," she told him, upset with his decree. "I'm a woman with no prospects for marrying."

"There is plenty of time for marriage." He sighed. "You must believe in yourself, Fannie." He descended the stairs. "I'll see you at home for supper."

She promised she'd follow her father

home after she said goodbye to David. Her father's declaration had stolen her good mood from dessert. Sighing, unhappy, she realized she'd overestimated her power to persuade her father. Although she thought he might not approve, she'd had high hopes for convincing him. Fannie had prayed that once he saw the space, he would agree that she could live there. Her luncheonette wasn't far from her father's house. She'd be safe living upstairs, wouldn't she? She honestly had wanted to live on her own.

She would make her *dat*'s favorite pie tomorrow. Maybe then he would forgive her for how she'd gone about this.

"What's wrong? What happened between you and your father?" David asked when she approached the table.

"My *vadder* and I have had a difference of opinion." She sighed. "Please don't ask. I can't talk about it right now."

Chapter Seventeen

Fannie was at the luncheonette as Robert Steele worked to replace the water heater since the unit came in quicker than he'd thought. When he left, he told her that he would be back soon to check the electric along with the air-conditioning and heating. To her relief, her and David's efforts to get rid of the water had saved her building from serious, long-lasting damage. They had turned off the electric fans when they'd left yesterday and put everything inside the kitchen to store. It wasn't safe to run a generator indoors, and she couldn't leave the back door open. Without David's help, she wouldn't have been able to store the generator in the building.

On Tuesday morning, she and her father pulled the generator outside and turned on the fans again.

"You might want to paint the dining room," her *dat* said after further inspection of the front room. Not a word was mentioned about the upstairs apartment. It was as if, having made himself clear on the subject, her *vadder* refused to discuss it.

Upset by the water damage, her father had ridden in the buggy with her to the restaurant first thing. He'd taken another long look at his surroundings. "I'll run to get paint. Why don't we ask DJ and Danny to help us?"

"I hate to bother them...and you." Fannie frowned as she felt the breeze from the fan. "You've already done too much." She hugged herself with her arms. It seemed chilly inside compared to the outside, although the air-conditioning couldn't run without power.

"You're my *dochter*, and they are your *bruders*," her father said, his expression softening. "Family helps and supports one another."

"Okey." Fannie studied the dining area's walls and baseboards. "If they can't make it, that's fine." She studied the tables and chairs. "I'd like to wait until after I scrub the walls and baseboards before we paint. I'd like to go over them with bleach water."

Her *dat* left to buy paint after discussing with her how much she'd need. Fannie gave him her credit card for the purchase, but he refused to take it.

"You've fed me more meals than I can count without taking a penny. I want to do this for you, Fannie. Let me...*please*."

Fannie gave in because what else could she do? And after all, it was only paint. It wasn't as if he would be paying for the repairs on the place.

The fans ran all day and into the evening. Her father dropped off the paint a half hour later along with a tank of fuel for the generator before he left to finish his chores on the dairy farm. Fannie stayed in the building until it was past supper when her twin brothers came to see her.

"Not much to paint," DJ said. "We're happy to help."

Danny nodded in agreement.

"Would you both do me a favor?" Fannie gazed up at them, loving that they were here for her. The two men, like her, were often busy with work, so the only time she could see her brothers was at Sunday church service and occasionally on Visiting Day. "I need to turn off the generator and pull it inside to protect it. It's a rental, and it's supposed to rain tonight."

"We'll handle it," Danny said.

Fannie thanked them and decided right then and there that she would cook up a storm for them and deliver it to their house. She'd wondered whether or not they ever enjoyed any home-cooked meals and later learned that they used takeout more often than not.

Mary stopped by after Fannie got home. "Fannie…*hallo*!"

Stunned to see her, Fannie smiled. "It's late. I'm surprised to see you."

"I would have been here earlier." David's sister smiled. "But I was at work. This morning David asked me to stop by. I was running behind and couldn't visit. I tried calling you, but you didn't answer."

"My phone was low on charge, so I turned it off. I switched it back for a quick charge before I left." Fannie moved to allow Mary's entry. "Come in."

"*Nay*, it's best if we talk out here. I need to get home to help Mam with supper." Mary waited for Fannie to step outside and close the door.

"How's the new job going?" Fannie asked.

Mary scowled. "Some days it's fine. On the other days, my new boss can be…difficult."

"Are you going to keep working there?"

"*Ja*, the pay is *gut*," Mary said. "And most of the time, everything is fine." She sighed. "About David... First, let me apologize for not getting here sooner. My *bruder* is going to be upset with me. He wanted to check to see how things are going. He's been worried. I couldn't believe it when he told me what happened with the water heater."

The mention of David's concern made Fannie feel warm and cared for. "Tell him I'm fine. My *dat* and *bruders* are going to help me paint after the plumber does his work tomorrow."

"That's *gut*." Mary hesitated. "How are your twin *bruders*?"

"They're fine." Fannie debated whether to ask after her brother. She'd wished for David to check on her all day, and she decided it was worthy of the embarrassment if Mary teased her. "David...is he *oll recht*?"

"You mean because he remembered that day? *Ja*, he's *okey*. He had a doctor's appointment today in New Wilmington with his neurologist." Mary rubbed her forehead, looking tired. "It's over four hours one way by car. Dat went with him, as he didn't want David to go alone. They're spending the night before they return by a hired car late tomorrow."

"I hope his visit went *oll recht*." Fannie couldn't help but be concerned about him. She felt better about why she hadn't seen him. She sent up a silent prayer that he received only good news from his doctor.

"I don't know how the doctor's visit and David's tests went yet. Dat said he'd call later this evening." Mary studied her wristwatch. "I have to go. Mam wants me to be close in case I get his call."

"*Danki* for stopping by, Mary. If you talk with David, please let him know I'm fine and that I'm thinking of him." At the curious look on Mary's face, Fannie quickly explained. "David helped me clean up on Monday. It was after…"

"You went with him to the police station." Mary smiled when Fannie bobbed her head. "That was *gut* of you to go."

"We became friends when we worked together on the reunion." Fannie felt her face heat and quickly glanced toward the house.

"I'll talk with you again soon." Mary waved then went to her buggy, climbed in and drove away. Fannie could still feel the heat in her cheeks because of the look Mary gave her when she'd claimed to be David's friend. And she was. At one time, there was more between them but that was years ago, and no one knew except her… Maybe someday David would remember, too.

"The news is *gut, soohn*. You have nothing to worry about." His father sat in a chair in their hotel room.

"Dr. Jax said it wasn't unusual for you to have memory loss with a head injury like yours. But after six months when you still couldn't remember…we continued to pray that eventually, it would return."

David paced the room as his father explained more than he wanted to know. It had already been a shock to hear this from the doctor but then to learn his family's side of the ordeal. He halted and faced Dat. "I'm sorry you had to go through that."

"You're the one who went through it, David. We hated how much you suffered. When you regained your memories about us and the attack, we had hope again. With the breakthrough, we knew it was important to call the neurologist. Dr. Jax was pleased and wanted to see you." His father beamed at him. "Your CT scan today confirmed that your brain has healed and there is no need to return to see him unless you suffer a new injury." His father stood and closed the distance between them, laying his hand on David's shoulder. "This is *wunderbor* news. You are yourself again. I'm so happy for you. I promised to call your sister so your *mudder* doesn't worry."

David nodded. "We can use the phone in the room." He was eager to get out of New Wilmington. The place held nothing but bad memories for him—now that he could remember them all. He'd been so nervous since coming here that he'd imagined seeing one of the men who had beaten him on the street near the doctor's office. He was more than ready to go home...and see Fannie again. He wondered how she was making out with the new water heater. The plumber was set to install it sometime today.

Dat sounded excited as he explained to his mother and siblings the outcome of David's doctor's visit. His father laughed, coaxing David's smile. Thank goodness he remembered his childhood and family. While David was happy with his memories of his past relationship with Fannie, he couldn't help wondering why she'd never mentioned what they once meant to each other. Was it because he'd hurt her badly when he'd left without a word? He shook his head. It didn't matter now. Fannie was his, and he would convince her. As soon as his attackers were in jail.

Dat hung up the phone and faced him

with happy tears in his eyes. "Your *schwe-schter* was thrilled to hear the news. I could hear your *mudder* cry out in the background before Mary put her on the phone."

David grinned. "I'm glad." He hesitated. "Now that we're done with the doctor, may we leave at first light? I'm eager to go home and away from here."

His *dat*'s expression grew somber. "I understand. I'll call Bert Hadley and let him know we'll be ready to leave at six."

"Danki." David was relieved. The Eng-lisher frequently gave rides to those in their Amish community. The man was also happy to be hired for long-distance trips like theirs to New Wilmington.

"Do you want to stop at the police sta-tion here on the way out?" his father asked. "Find out if there is any news?"

"Nay." The last thing David wanted was to stay in New Wilmington a moment lon-ger—and he didn't want to relive that day one more time. "Officer Michaels in New

Berne said he'd let me know as soon as any of the three men are apprehended."

"Fine, *soohn*." Dat smiled. "Then we'll keep to the plan and head straight home first thing in the morning. Let's get some supper, *ja*? There is a restaurant downstairs."

David was overly conscious of the expense of this trip. "I'll pay you back, Dat."

His father arched his eyebrows. "You're my *soohn*. There is nothing to pay back."

They arrived home the next day by late morning. David was eager to see Fannie and check in with her. But as he followed his father inside the house, Mam rushed forward to hug him with the biggest smile on her face. He knew then that he would have to stay close to the house for the rest of the day. He'd have to wait until tomorrow to see how Fannie and her business were faring.

During the night, David decided to contact Amos Mast, who had hired him as his apprentice before he'd left New Berne two years ago. He wanted to talk with him about returning to work and his apprenticeship. He prayed the man would forgive him for leaving the way he did and agree.

After breakfast, he drove to the workshop of the cabinetmaker. The more he thought about the prospect of working with Amos again, the more pleased he was. Once all three criminals were caught and jailed, he would finally have his chance to win back Fannie Miller. His chosen trade would be a way to provide for her and the family they would create together after they wed…if he could convince her to give him another chance first.

On Wednesday morning, Robert Steele checked the electrical outlets in all areas of the restaurant to make sure they were safe as well as the air-conditioning and heating unit. Then he flipped on the main circuit breaker and switched on all the lights in the hallway, kitchen, closet and dining room.

Fannie hadn't seen nor spoken with David since Monday. She understood that he'd been out of town for a doctor's visit. How were his scans? Was he all right? Or did the doctor find something else wrong with him? She couldn't help but worry.

She'd spent the days since Monday cleaning the floor with a disinfectant that had a bleach additive to fight mold and mildew. Although it was summer, once the electricity was on again, she turned on the heat rather than the AC to make sure the rooms were fully dry and there were no long-term effects from the water. Robert Steele had completed the work, and Fannie had written him a check for everything she owed him, grimacing inwardly at her severely reduced bank balance. She took comfort that once she opened Fannie's again, she'd be able to add funds to increase both her savings and checking accounts.

Her thoughts centered on David, who was never out of her mind. She missed him. Fannie knew she had no right to spend time with him. They were friends. After the work they had done for the reunion together, the support they had given each other when one of them was scared or hurting, she couldn't help praying for more with him.

She'd given up on the idea of living in the upstairs apartment. Her father had been adamant in his refusal to allow her to reside there, and she wouldn't disobey him. Her father had done too much for her and her siblings not to give him the respect he deserved.

On Thursday, her brothers showed up with her father midmorning, carrying paintbrushes, rollers and tarps, all equipment they must have picked up on the way.

Dat handed her a lunch pail. "Figured you'd be hungry about now."

She opened it up to see a sandwich, a bag of chips and a plum. *"Danki."* Fannie smiled. "I can make you all something for lunch—the power is back on."

"Maybe later," Danny said. "Let's get started in the dining room." Her brother captured her gaze. "No need for you to paint today. We have it covered."

"Danny—"

Their father agreed. "He's right, *dochter*. I'm sure you need to do an inventory of your supplies before you reopen." He grinned. "And do you think you could find us something to snack on while we work?"

"How about a chocolate peanut butter pie?" Fannie saw the smiles that brightened each of their faces. While they worked, she decided it was a good time to take inventory of what supplies she had and what she'd need to purchase. She stopped at the grocery store to stock up on new ingredients. Then she returned to the luncheonette and got to work on the pie, collecting unsweetened cocoa, baking powder, bread flour and confectioners' sugar from her stores. As she sifted the dry ingredients, she wondered if David was home. Would he come by to see her? Dealing with the mess in her luncheonette and missing David, she battled tears and a lump in her throat.

She took solace in the one thing that had helped her when David had gone away—creating food.

The pie shell was in the oven. Fannie was preparing the chocolate peanut butter filling before she made the whipped cream topping. She heard the back door open and close but didn't move. Her father or one of her brothers must have gone to buy more paint. The timer went off, and she pulled the piecrust from the oven and set it to cool on a rack. Curious as to how the dining room was looking, she left the kitchen for the dining room and heard her father talking. Good, her *dat* was back. She called out to him.

The voice that answered, however, didn't belong to her father. It was David's.

Chapter Eighteen

David had finally made it to Fannie's Luncheonette. When he walked in, he heard voices in the dining area. He grinned when he saw Jonas Miller and his identical twin sons, DJ and Danny, painting the walls and baseboards. With fresh paint, the room had a brand-new look. There was no sign of any water damage or dampness anywhere. The floor appeared fine, although he had no idea how.

"It looks *gut*," he commented as he entered the room.

"David!" Jonas glanced over with a smile. "It's slowly coming along. Shouldn't be too long before Fannie's can open again." He wiped his cheek with the back of his hand, leaving a small smear of white paint.

Pointing toward the man's face, David laughed. "I didn't realize your cheek was a part of this painting job." He met each of the brothers' gazes. "DJ. Danny. Nice to see you. I'm sorry I couldn't get back here to help sooner."

"It's fine. We have it handled," Danny said. "I heard what you did when you found this mess. *Danki* for being there for my *schweschter* when she needed you."

"I planned to come back on Tuesday," David told them, "but I had no idea my *mudder* made a doctor's appointment for me in New Wilmington. Dat and I stayed overnight and came back yesterday."

Fannie's father studied him with concern. "Did your appointment go well?"

David realized that as a preacher, Jonas had known what had happened and the reason behind his visit to his neurologist.

"It did. I don't have to go back. I've been released."

Jonas beamed at him. "Congratulations."

Movement out of the corner of his eye heralded Fannie's presence. He turned and flashed her a grin. "The luncheonette looks *wunderbor*. I'm happy for you."

Her expression serious, Fannie nodded. "We're slowly getting there." She continued to study him intently. "Your appointment went well," she said as if she'd overheard the conversation between him and her father.

"*Ja*. Praise the Lord." David caught the shuttered look on her face and wondered what was wrong. "It's been a long time coming."

"I'm glad for you." Her smile was weak, yet Fannie seemed sincere.

David felt the urgent need to speak with her alone. "Would you walk outside with me for a moment? I'd like to talk with you." Fannie glanced at her father, who nodded. She thought they were friends only, but he had other plans for her…if he could get her to forgive him.

He stepped outside and Fannie followed. David faced her with a wary look once they were alone. "Fannie, I wanted to come sooner to help. There's been—" he stared at the ground "—a lot going on."

He watched her expression soften. "Did you hear from Officer Michaels?"

He shook his head. "I wish." He captured her hand and tugged her farther away from the building. "Fannie, I need to tell you about my injuries. You know that I've struggled with amnesia, but you don't know exactly why." David leaned back. "When I was beaten, I suffered severe head trauma. I needed surgery to reduce the pressure in my brain caused by blood filling the area beneath my skull. The doctor warned my parents that I might suffer lasting damage." He inhaled sharply, recalling a time that had been frightening for him. "When I recalled the attack, it was a breakthrough for me. Dr. Jax wanted me to come into his office, and I had a CT scan. The news was *gut*. My brain looked normal, and I've been discharged from Dr. Jax's care."

Fannie gazed at him with awe. "That's *wunderbor*, David. You must be grateful and relieved."

David nodded. "I am. Except I felt terrible that I couldn't be here to help you with what needed to be done. I asked Mary to let you know where I'd gone. And then first thing this morning, I went for a job interview. I'm an apprentice again for Amos Mast. I asked him if he would take me back, and after learning what had happened to me, he was happy to rehire me."

She smiled. "That's *gut*, *ja*?"

"*Ja.*" He returned her smile. "I start work this coming Monday. So until then, would you let me help you get ready for the reopening of your restaurant? I can start by painting the hallway." He pleaded with his eyes, hope filling him. "Please?"

Looking uncertain, Fannie appeared

deep in thought and then nodded. "Talk with my *vadder*. I don't know what his plans are for painting. He's determined to help me. Dat said he wouldn't take *nay* for an answer when it came to his desire to paint and do other repair work."

"I will." David grinned. "*Danki.* I won't interfere if he doesn't want me here. Everything is already looking brand-new. Your customers, including me, will be excited when you open your doors again."

He studied Fannie's expression and worried that she was acting more reserved with him and less happy to include him in her life. "Fannie?" he said. "We're friends, aren't we?"

After a moment of hesitation, she bobbed her head. "*Ja*, friends."

David experienced an uncomfortable feeling. Something had changed between them. He wanted desperately to tell her that he remembered their relationship, especially the day he'd confessed his love. While he couldn't tell her the truth yet for her protection, he'd prayed that she'd keep seeing him as a friend until the danger was gone and he was free to pursue her.

Jonas's sons were done for the day. David spoke with Fannie's father about painting the hallway. Jonas seemed happy to have David work with him.

"There is no sign of mold or mildew," David noted with surprise.

Jonas smiled. "Fannie wiped everything down with disinfectant and a solution that prevents mold."

It didn't take him and Jonas long to finish the narrow space. Fannie stayed in the kitchen while he and her father worked together. She came out once to check on their progress and spoke with her father but not with him. It hurt that she'd chosen to ignore him. A feeling of dread burned in his stomach. Would he be able to rebuild their relationship to what it had been before?

As he left the restaurant later that day, David couldn't stop worrying about his future with Fannie. He didn't want to lose her. His attackers needed to be found and arrested soon so he could woo Fannie, get her to trust him and convince her he would never leave her again. She needed to know how much he loved her, but he was afraid that she wouldn't forgive him for breaking her heart—however unintentional. He feared that he'd never have everything that he wanted with the woman he loved—Fannie in his life as his wife and the mother of his children.

Please, Lord, help us find our way... bless our union so that we can wed and live together in Your light and love... Amen.

Anxious, David decided to visit the police station to ask if his attackers had been arrested yet. He needed to do something fast. He wanted to protect Fannie, but he couldn't lose her by waiting too long to tell her that he loved her.

He steered his buggy toward the other side of town and pulled into the lot next to the police station. David parked and tied his horse to the hitching post before he entered the building. Officer Michaels was at the front desk.

David approached him. "Hello. I—"

"David," the officer said with a smile. "I was going to get in touch with you."

"Yes?" The fact that the man appeared pleased gave David hope.

"Dennis Porter and two of his known associates have been picked up and arrested. They've been charged with assault and battery and first-degree murder." Michaels invited David to follow him into the back room. "Have a seat."

The man pulled out a different mug book and flipped open to a particular page. "Do any of these men look familiar?"

David nodded as he studied the mug shots. He recognized his attackers and saw a third man with the same last name.

"They were much younger in this photo," the officer said. "These two are the Benedetto brothers—Ralphie and

Georgie. And this man?" He gestured toward another photo. "He's the one who was murdered. During interrogation, Porter ignored his attorney's advice and confessed that it was because of a drug deal gone bad. He must have thought he'd receive a lesser sentence if he talked. According to him, the victim had chickened out and didn't want to be involved anymore. His name was Pauly Benedetto, their youngest brother, who threatened to go to the police if they didn't stop dealing." Michaels touched Pauly's mug shot and shook his head. "Cold murderers if they can kill their own brother. Dennis and the remaining Benedetto brothers deserve a life sentence."

David shuddered as he recalled the terror of that awful day. "Will I have to testify at their trial? And what if there were others involved?" Would he ever feel safe again?

Officer Michaels studied him with understanding. "It's possible that the sketches and an affidavit about what you saw and endured will be enough for the trial. But I can't guarantee it."

"Are my family and friends in danger?" David asked.

"I was told these thugs are low-level dealers, who apparently tried to score on their own. It's doubtful they told anyone about the drugs or what they did to you and to Pauly." He picked up the mug book. "I'll get in touch with the prosecuting attorney in New Wilmington and let you know what I find out."

He gazed at the officer with hope in his heart. "Thank you." David gave him the number for Kings General Store. "If I'm not there, please leave a message and I'll return your call."

"I will," the officer promised. "In the meantime, relax. Porter and the Benedettos will be arraigned this week." Michaels closed the book and put it on a shelf. "Have faith in the system."

"Thank you," David said. "Thanks for believing me."

"You should thank that girl of yours," he replied. "She's the one who pushed me to check out your story. I'm sorry I needed the push. We have people who come in with stories that never pan out...and your report was for a crime that happened over two years ago."

David felt excited as he headed home. He felt relaxed and happy for the first time since he'd awakened in the hospital. The officer was right. He had Fannie to thank for convincing the police to start an investigation. *And for making me feel free.*

If he had to testify, he would. But he refused to be afraid any longer. He would prove to Fannie that he remembered her, loved her and wanted her forever in his life.

As he drove past Kings General Store, he decided to purchase a special treat in celebration. He went to the bakery section and bought seven éclairs. As he handed over the cash to Jed King, the phone rang.

The call was from New Berne Police Department. Jed handed him the phone. "I was lucky and got a hold of the district attorney," Officer Michaels said. "Because of what you went through, he is willing to accept an affidavit. If, for some reason, he changes his mind and you have to testify, you'll be in closed quarters with only the judge and attorneys from both sides. Either way your identity will be protected."

"Thank you," David said before he hung up with a sigh of relief.

The bells on the front entrance jingled. Amos Mast, his new employer and expert cabinetmaker, walked into the store. "David! I was going to stop by your *haus*. I know we agreed on Monday for you to start work again, but do you think you could come in tomorrow? I can use your help. My *soohn* can't work, and I have a client who wants a dresser delivered by the weekend."

David studied the kind man who'd agreed to take him on as an apprentice again. Grateful for the second chance, he didn't hesitate, although he was disappointed that he wouldn't get to spend time with Fannie until the weekend. "I'll be happy to help. Seven thirty still *gut*? Or do you need me to come in earlier to meet your deadline?"

"Seven thirty is fine." Amos looked pleased. "I'm looking forward to having you in the shop again."

"I am, too. I remember everything you taught me." David took the bagged éclairs and left for home. He had so much for which to be thankful, and he was.

Fannie spent Friday preparing for the reopening of her luncheonette on Monday. It was late afternoon, and she hadn't seen David all day. So, when she heard someone enter through the back door, she froze. David?

"Fannie?" It was her father. "Do you need any help or are you all set?"

"Everything is ready, Dat, thanks to you." *And DJ, Danny and David.* "How is everything at the farm?" She knew he'd been busy all day with his dairy farm. The young man who had been helping him, Nate Hostetler, had to visit a sick cousin up north in Pennsylvania, a place in Indiana County called Smicksburg.

Her *dat* smiled. "Things are fine. I did all my chores and have a bit of time until I'm back at it again."

"I'm ready for Monday's opening." She glanced around the kitchen, pleased at what she saw. "It's *okey* for you to go home. I'll follow you in a minute."

Her father nodded, gave her a hug and left.

Fannie locked up and then headed home. As she passed Kings General Store, she saw David leaving with a shopping bag.

She sighed with regret. David had yet to remember what they'd once had together. She was saddened that he wanted friendship and nothing more.

Saturday morning, she baked and cooked to prepare a feast to celebrate the upcoming reopening of Fannie's. Now that the work at her luncheonette was done, her father seemed upset with her about the apartment again. He probably thought she was eager to get away from him, which wasn't true. At times, she'd felt out of place living in the house with the newlyweds, but not now. Her father made sure that she was wanted and loved. Alta made her feel that way, too. So, she would continue to live here…until she was twenty-nine. Then she would push to move out, for it wouldn't be right for a spinster to live under her father's roof.

Tomorrow, she and her parents would visit Deacon Thomas and his family. Fannie prepared a bowl of coleslaw, and Alta made an upside-down chocolate cake.

Sunday morning, the three of them climbed into the family buggy and headed toward Deacon Thomas's house. Her father seemed to have fully forgiven her, for which Fannie sent up a silent prayer of thanks.

It was only as her father steered his horse next to the deacon's barn that Fannie knew for certain that David Troyer and his family were visiting the deacon, too. She watched as the Troyers' buggy pulled in to park next to them. Fannie grabbed the bowl of coleslaw and hurried toward the house.

"Fannie!" It was David.

She halted and breathed deeply as she waited for him to reach her. She couldn't help the joy she felt upon seeing him. "David." Fannie gave him a nod.

He looked excited, his blue eyes sparkling, his smile wide. "I need to talk with you later."

Fannie stared at him. "You seem…"

"Happy?" David bobbed his head. "I am. They arrested those men."

She couldn't help smiling. Fannie was glad he was safe.

"Will you walk with me before lunch? There are things I want to share with you." He eyed her with a puppy dog expression.

How could she resist? She loved David. After believing that heartbreak had cured her of her love for him, it hadn't. How could she stay angry after learning about everything he'd endured? She might have felt broken after he'd left without a word and hadn't returned until two years later, but David was the one who had suffered. He'd suffered worse than she had. He'd lost his memory, his life, his family...everything. Even her, she realized. Because he still couldn't remember how much they'd meant to each other.

"Fannie? I won't take too much of your time."

She released a breath and smiled. "*Okey.* Just come find me when you want to talk."

"How about you put that coleslaw in the *haus* and then take a walk with me?" David bit his lip as he waited for her answer.

"Oll recht." She brought the bowl into the house. When she returned outside, she approached where David waited for her. He set those intense blue eyes on her and grinned. Fannie was stunned by how excited and happy he looked. She stopped to tell Alta where she was going. Alta glanced toward David briefly and nodded. Fannie saw a young unfamiliar woman with blond hair in the yard, chatting with Jed and Rachel King. "Do you know who that girl is?" Fannie asked as she reached David's side.

He got a funny look on his face. "That's Hannah Lapp from Happiness. She's Rachel's cousin."

"You've met?" Fannie felt a tightening in her chest.

David nodded. "My *mam* introduced us this morning."

"I see." She followed the man who had always held a special place in her heart from the first moment they'd become friends and then something more four years ago.

Was Hannah the reason that David didn't want to be more than friends with her? She was being ridiculous. Fannie swallowed hard. There was a reason he wanted her to walk with him. Hopefully a good one.

David couldn't wait to get her alone. He needed to tell her about the arrests, what Officer Michaels had said, but mostly what he remembered about him and her. Would she forgive him for not getting in touch? He had planned to do it all along, but then his grandfather had been so sick...and the next morning he'd been attacked.

He led her to the row of vehicles parked alongside the barn. He'd come by himself. When his family had arrived, he'd gone to help them.

Fannie must not have realized that he'd driven by himself, for she looked stunned when he'd brought her to his pony cart. "David? I thought we were going for a walk."

"We are." He helped her up into his cart. She gazed down at him with a look of confusion. "Trust me." He saw her swallow hard. "It's... You'll see."

He had brought the cart for the sole purpose of finding time alone with Fannie. He had worked all day on Friday, and then yesterday he'd worked with his father, who'd needed help in his workshop. Now that the time was here to confess everything to the woman he loved, he was suddenly scared. *What if she doesn't understand? What if she rejects my request to court her?*

Fannie was quiet as he drove. When he pulled into the lot behind her restaurant, she shifted in her seat, causing him to glance at her, to make sure she was all right. He parked in the back of the lot near the outbuilding. David hopped out and then offered his hand to assist her.

She studied him warily. "David—"

"Trust me, Fannie," he urged as he helped her down. "I know you might find it hard, but please trust me."

She nodded. "I don't understand. What are we doing here?" She seemed surprised when he didn't let go of her hand.

He smiled at her and pointed toward the back of the property. He led her through a grassy area beyond the lot and continued until they reached a path in the woods that bordered the field. The shade was lovely, but he particularly enjoyed the way the sunlight found its way through the foliage to light up the trail ahead. Then he reached the exact spot he wanted…a sunny clearing near a stream. There was a large rock to the right close to the water. David heard Fannie gasp as he held her hand and pulled her toward it.

"David," she breathed. "Is this?"

"*Ja*, Fannie. It's the place where I first

told you that I loved you. When I asked if I could court you." He closed his eyes on a wave of pain. "I remember you, Fannie. I know us, and I would like to start again. Please let me court you."

Fannie squeezed his hand. "When did you know?"

"I didn't just recall the attack," he whispered. "I remembered everything. I knew *you*."

She frowned and withdrew her hand from his grasp. "Why didn't you tell me?"

"Because before late Thursday afternoon, I couldn't be sure that you'd stay safe." He reached for both of her hands. "I received some *wunderbor* news. My attackers are in jail and will be arraigned this week. I have no idea when the trial will be, but I refuse to let it upset me any longer. Officer Michaels said the court might accept an affidavit of my account about what happened and how I suffered afterward." He gently squeezed her fingers, enjoying the connection. "I may not have to testify in court but if I do, I'll be alone with the judge and the lawyers."

"That's *wunderbor.*" She looked happy for him.

"You are *wunderbor,* Fannie Miller." He pulled her to sit on the rock beside him. "I love you and want to marry you. Let me court you the way I should have been able to two years ago."

"I don't know." She had tears in her eyes. "I'm afraid. I was heartbroken when you left and didn't come back. I don't know if I can risk it. And what about Fannie's Luncheonette?"

"Fannie, you must know by now that I didn't leave you willingly. I never will. I had every intention of letting you know where I was, but then the attack happened..." He wanted nothing more than to pull her into his arms. "I want to have a family with you. And as for Fannie's... I don't expect you to give up your restaurant. I'm so proud of what you've accomplished, and I'd be happy to help if you'll let me." David swallowed hard, feeling emotional. "Please allow me to court you. I promise I won't let you down."

"And if we marry and have children?" she asked.

"Your employees can take over until you're ready to go back to work." David felt her hands tremble and held on to them tenderly. "Fannie, trust me. Take a chance on me. You won't regret it." He drew a breath. "I know I hurt you when I left."

Fannie blinked back tears as she nodded. "You did."

"You have to believe that I'd never willingly leave you, Fannie. Ever."

"*Gut*, because I could never go through that again." Her expression softened. "How long of a courtship?"

"Three months until the month of weddings in November. I'll help you with Fannie's whenever I'm not making furniture with Amos Mast." He gazed into her blue eyes, loving her features, her heart…everything about her. "We can be married after the banns are read in church for three weeks." Notice of the upcoming marriage would be read to ensure that no one objects to the union.

Her hesitation turned to a look of joy intermingled with amusement. "That doesn't seem like much time."

"We are already two years too late, love. Let me court you and then marry you in three months." David waited with worry for Fannie's answer.

"Court me if you wish, but as for marrying you?" Fannie paused and his heart wondered if it would stop beating. "*Ja*, I'll marry you, David Troyer... In three months. Tomorrow. Anytime at all." She bit her lip. "We can live in the apartment above Fannie's, if you want, until we find a house of our own."

"You have an apartment upstairs?" He raised his brows in surprise.

"*Ja*. And my *dat* wasn't happy to learn about it." She gave him a wry smile. "There isn't much up there. Just a bathroom with a shower. But there is room for a bed, and I can do the cooking in the commercial kitchen downstairs."

"You agreed to be my wife. Praise and thank the Lord." David's heart overflowed with love. He rose and tugged her into his arms for a hug, one he'd lived too long without. "I'll be happy wherever we live as long as I'm with you."

Epilogue

Five Years Later

Four-year-old Rose Troyer watched her father as he painted a clear but shiny liquid on the cradle he'd crafted in his shop. He dipped the brush in a can, wiped it against the inside edge and carefully spread the mixture over the light-colored wood.

"What're you doing, Dat?" She enjoyed spending time in his workshop in the backyard where he built furniture. Rose had once asked him why he didn't have a dairy farm like her grandfather, and her father had said that he loved making things with his hands, furniture that made people happy in their homes. Rose never forgot his answer. Her father smiled a lot, and he made her smile a lot, too.

His eyes were soft as he studied her. "I'm putting a protective coating on this cradle."

"Who's the cradle for?" They already had the one that used to be hers when she was a baby. She wondered why he was making this one.

"Us," he said. "Because we'll need it soon." Dat finished painting and put the lid on the can, which he tapped into place with a hammer.

Rose was confused. "We have a cradle."

"But we need another one." He picked her up and held her in his arms. "Soon, Rosie, we'll have two new babies in the house. You'll be a big sister to two baby boys."

"Bruders?" Two of them? Rose wasn't sure how she felt about having brothers instead of sisters, but she supposed Mam

might need her to help take care of them. So, that would be all right.

"*Ja, bruders,*" Dat said with a wide grin as his gaze lit up with happiness. "Twins." He set her down. "They could be identical." He ruffled her hair, which she knew was already coming loose from its bobby pins.

"Like Mam's *bruders*—Onkel Danny and Onkel DJ."

"That's *recht.*"

Her mother had a big belly. When Rose had asked why, Mam explained to her that she was carrying a baby. It wasn't until now that she found out that there were two of them.

Her father was studying the cradle. Wasn't it done? It looked finished to her.

"Dat?" Rose tugged on the fabric of his shirt.

"*Ja?*" He seemed preoccupied as he re-opened the big can and dipped the brush inside again.

"How does Mam get those babies out of her belly?" she asked, blinking up at him.

Dat froze as he looked down at her. "When it's time, *Gott* makes it happen."

She nodded. Rose knew that God provided when a church member needed something and that He blessed couples who wanted to get married. *Gott can do anything.*

"Do you want lunch?" Rose continued to watch her father work.

"In a few minutes," he responded, his attention consumed with his brushstrokes on the cradle.

"I'm going to tell Mam that we'll be hungry soon," Rose declared.

"*Gut* idea, little *dochter.* Tell her I'll be ready to eat in a half hour."

Rose ran to the house and burst through the kitchen doorway. She loved their home. There was a bedroom that was hers alone and another one besides the one that Mam and Dat slept in. *That must be where my bruders will sleep.* She recalled the day that her father had put the one cradle they already had there. A room for her *bubbel bruders*.

"Mam?" Rosie expected her mother to be in the kitchen but she wasn't there. "Mudder!"

Her *mam* entered the room. She looked pale as she clutched her stomach. "Rose," she gasped. "Get Dat. Tell him I need him."

Rose was suddenly scared. "Mam—"

"Go tell him, *dochter*." Mam pulled out a chair and held on to its back.

Rose ran out to her father's workshop. "Dat!"

"*Ja*, Rosie?" He appeared distracted.

"Mam's in the kitchen. She needs you."

"Tell her I'll be right there."

"*Nay*, Dat! She needs you now! I think she's sick. She's holding on to her belly!"

Her father threw down the brush before he rushed out of the building and toward the house. Rose ran after him. When she got inside, she saw Dat with his arms around Mam while he murmured to her soothingly. He then made a call on Mam's cell phone and hung up.

"Dat?" Rose was scared. There was an urgency about the call and her parents' behavior. What was happening?

Her *dat* smiled at her, although he looked tense. "The babies are coming, Rosie."

"*Gott* is getting them out today?"

"*Ja,*" her *mam* said with a smile that turned into a grimace as she clutched her belly.

A knock resounded on the screen door. It was Bert, the man who sometimes gave her family rides. Rose opened the door. "*Gott* is going to give me my *bubbel bruders* today."

The big Englisher with the bright, colorful marks across his arms stood on their stoop and grinned. "Aren't you lucky that today is the day?"

Before Rose could respond, her father was helping her mother out of the house and into Bert's car. "Dat?" She didn't want to be left behind.

Dat took one look at her expression. "Let me get your *mam* settled in the back seat. You can sit up front with Bert."

Rose obeyed and got into the car. She prayed hard as Bert drove fast and finally pulled into the parking lot of the hospital. Swiveling to eye her parents, she gazed at them with tears in her eyes.

"Don't worry, Rosie," her father assured her with a smile. "Soon, you'll get to see Mam with your *bruders.*"

She sat in the waiting room with Bert until the Englisher left after Grossdaddi Jonas and Grossmammi Alta arrived to stay with her.

"Grossdaddi?" Rose reached out to touch her grandfather's arm. "Will my *mam* be *oll recht*?"

He patted her hand. "She'll be fine." Rose relaxed when she saw her grandmother bobbing her head in agreement.

"Who's going to take care of Fannie's?" she asked.

"Cousins Esther and Linda—and Hannah Lapp, who has come back for another visit."

It seemed like forever before her father came out through the double doors to the back of the hospital. "They're here. My sons are here and they each have ten fingers and ten toes."

"Congratulations, *soohn*," Grossdaddi Jonas said.

Grossmammi Alta smiled. "Congratulations, David."

Dat's gaze zoomed in on Rose. "In a few moments, you'll see Mam and meet your new little *bruders*."

Rose nodded. "*Gott* was successful in getting the babies out then?"

The three adults she knew and loved laughed. "*Ja.* He was successful," her father said before he went back through those huge wooden doors.

A short while later, Dat came out again and took her hand. Rose was nervous as he brought her through those doors to an area the likes of which she'd never seen before.

Mam was lying in a bed, holding two tiny babies in her arms. Rose approached quietly with her heartbeat hammering in her chest. Her mother's smile was wide. "Come and see your twin *bruders*," she said.

Rose realized that her grandparents waited patiently by the door as she moved to the bed to see the babies.

"Jonas Jonathan and Joshua Samuel." Mam smiled over her head at Rose's grandparents.

"Do we have to call them by both names?" Rose frowned when everyone laughed.

"*Nay*, Rosie," her father said as he picked her up in his arms. "We'll use Jonas or JJ and Joshua or Josh."

"They look the same," she said. "How will we tell them apart?"

Dat chuckled. "We'll figure it out."

"Will they look like you or Mam?" Rose studied them, wondering. She knew she looked like her *mam* with her blond hair and blue eyes. But her blue eyes could have come from her *mam* or her *dat*, Grossdaddi Jonas had once told her.

Rose watched the way Dat looked at her mother and how Mam gazed back at him. And she sighed. Her parents loved her and her brothers, but the love between her parents made her feel good. It was like the sun that seemed to grow brighter each day. She hoped someday she would find a man to love her like her father loved her mother. But she wasn't in a hurry. Because she was happy with her family, including her new baby brothers.

* * * * *